CLOUD 913

Also by Marko Joensuu:

The Red Scorpion:
The True Story of a Ruthless Russian Mob Boss's
Dramatic Redemption
(with Rami Kivisalo)

CLOUD 913
BOOK ONE OF THE TIME ROLL

MARKO JOENSUU

IHERINGIUS

First published in Great Britain by Iheringius

ISBN 978-0-9575354-0-4

A CIP catalogue record for this book is available from the British Library.

Iheringius
An imprint of
Joensuu Media Ltd
145-157 St John Street
London
EC1V 4PW
England

www.iheringius.com

DEDICATION

Thanks to my son Joshua who helped me discover my long-lost creativity, and to my wife Daniella without whose patience this book would never have been made possible. Also, without you, it wouldn't have been worth the effort.

1.

Robert Kelvin strolled its way past the tourists jamming the station entrance. When it stepped inside it observed a thermal drop of fifteen degrees. It closed its sweat pores. It scanned the faces of the people, looked for the police and security agents.

Everything looked *normal*.

It had one objective, one course of action. It had factored in the behavioural patterns of the commuters, based on the data from the mornings of the last two years, discounting any special events, and even now it kept updating the database.

Not that it made any difference.

An individual could act randomly but a crowd was always predictable.

It didn't feel nervous, not to the least.

Its timing was perfect; it always was. It caught the tail end of a cleaning turtle and followed it through the service gate. As a relic from some ancient trade union battles, the service gates were still operated by humans, and they were the easiest if not the only way to penetrate the security. Nothing ever happened there, and the guards were more interested in watching extreme robot fighting or whatever ticked their fancy than doing their job.

What was their job? It had managed to calculate everything else but that one had come back unresolved.

The guard took a quick, casual look at its workman's overalls, and the toolbox, and let it pass. It didn't see the reading in the gate's iris scanner but it knew that London Transport had just registered the entrance of Robert Kelvin, age thirty-five, an electrician who had worked for the underground's maintenance contractor for seven years, two months and fifteen days.

"About time to get them doors fixed," the guard said.

"Sorry for the wait," it responded. It spoke with a broad East London accent that resembled Old Cockney, a dialect that had very little to do with the east of the metropolis but came from the subculture of the manual labourers.

"The budget cuts have screwed up the level of service. You should vote for Tommy Henderson when it's time for the next mayor's elections. He stands for the working man."

The budgets were always cut but they always went up.

It monitored the guard's face and body for signs of suspicion or discomfort but didn't find any. His name was Kevin McCartney, he was forty-seven and he still lived with his mother in a small apartment in Brixton. His only friends came through work but even they laughed at him behind his back. Not the robots, though.

"Have a nice day!" it said and headed towards the escalator and the platforms.

There was an increase in temperature at the escalators, three and half degrees. It didn't move, not even when the office rats sped past it. There was no rush; it was on schedule. When it got to the platform it passed the service doors that needed fixing.

The train arrived in thirty-five seconds. The doors opened. It stepped in and took one of the seven vacant seats in the carriage, next to an old Englishman in a suit that had been out of fashion for two hundred and fifty years. Harry Windsor, eighty-seven, was an Eleventh Gulf War veteran, decorated with the Victoria Circle, the highest military decoration awarded for valour in battle, a medal he earned by saving the lives of fifteen soldiers, a career soldier forgotten by the government soon after the investiture held at Buckingham Palace fifty-three years, two months and three days ago.

It waited for thirty-seven seconds, until the train was deep in the tunnel. There was no wire to pull, no button to press, no tension, no sound. It merely *willed* and a few fractions of a second later after that, it felt nothing, absolutely nothing.

Nearly 314 years earlier Richard Holmes, a British archaeologist, stood at the plateau of Aregue in the northwest of Ethiopia, and watched the flood of Abyssinian warriors descend from the hills. It was four months since the British warships had landed on the shore and another five years from the beginning of the hostage crisis. In between, there had been four years of governmental heel-dragging, political manoeuvring, trade-offs, and relentless lobbying by the arms manufacturers. Like most wars, this one would have been completely avoidable had there been any interest in understanding the other party but once the forces of war had gathered momentum there was no stopping them.

War was good business.

The mobilisation had been extensive. There were well over ten thousand British soldiers between the Red Sea and the plateau of Aregue, more than enough to deal with the Emperor Tewodros' fifty thousand brave but ill-equipped warriors. It was a large army and perfectly capable of winning the war.

It wasn't here yet.

The main bulk of the troops lagged fifteen miles behind, the rest scattered along the hundred-mile trek between the highlands and the sea. The first group of thousand soldiers had withstood a four-month journey plagued by cholera, extreme heat, hard labour, thirst and occasional lack of food. They were hardly fit for battle.

Richard lifted the heavy binoculars that had served him well in Egypt and Persia and zoomed onto the mass of dark bodies nearing them on horseback. He could see their muskets and spears, machinery of war that was quite out of date but still capable of killing a man.

He dropped the binoculars and looked left and right, at the regiment. This was a surprise attack and yet it had taken them less than half a minute to form a defensive battle line.

The distance to the mass of black bodies was now around two hundred yards.

The rifles were raised but no one shot yet.

The regiment was one disciplined bunch.

There was one hundred yards between the British soldiers and the Abyssinians.

The galloping was already shaking the ground under his black, dusty boots.

The distance was now fifty yards.

The soldiers lifted their rifles, ready to shoot.

The breech-loading Sniders had never been tested in battle. They were the first ever batch manufactured in the factories of Enfield, near London.

The roaring from a thousand rifles shooting nearly simultaneously deafened his ears.

The first line of Abyssinians fell from the horseback. Their horses collided with each other. The first round was followed by the second.

Still, they kept on coming.

The Emperor must have known that he would lose the first wave of the warriors but he would have estimated it to take a lot longer for the British soldiers to reload. He couldn't have known that the new rifles were capable of shooting ten rounds a minute, eight more than any other rifle.

Two hours later, climbing up the hill and trying not to step over the bodies of the Abyssinian warriors, the words of a friend, a career officer, came to his mind.

"Sometimes it is difficult to carry out very difficult orders, but even though the command recognises this, they will not admit their mistake until every man has died trying to carry them out." There had been a resigned expression on his face; he hadn't quite grasped what it signified, not until now.

The Emperor Tewodros was known for his wasteful lifestyle and even at his death he kept on wasting, now people.

It took Richard nearly half an hour to clean his boots from bloodstains when he finally got on top of the mountain.

2.

Nathan had been on the street level barely a minute but the back of his shirt was already soaking in sweat. It was only a few days after Midsummer and London was at its most scorching. Regardless, he stuck with cotton shirts as he disliked the feel of the self-cooling fabrics. He hadn't taken any anti-sweat medication either.

He would rather sweat.

It was possible to walk from Euston to King's Circle via one of the air-conditioned tunnels but that would have meant missing the pre-Do-Muzude architecture that gave the Borough of Camden its distinctive atmosphere. He took a few steps left to avoid the cleaning turtle sweeping the station hall and nearly knocked down a shabby-looking, pony-tailed senior citizen in an orange self-cooling suit.

"Sorry for the inconvenience," the turtle said with a perfectly constructed apologetic line that admitted neither responsibility nor liability.

"Watch it, dickhead!" the ponytail said. Nathan pretended he didn't hear that and followed him to the escalator.

"Get your WearStocks! Now with self-healing micro-rays!"

The advertising screen reacted to the passing of a trader in a pinstripe suit. Although he looked young, barely over twenty, his pair was old and worn. They were chunky, concealed the nose and not just the eyes. The side effects of those early models were flashbacks and visual confusion disorders. Most traders got rid of them as soon as they could afford a new one but for new trainees they provided a cheap entry point to trading.

Nathan touched his wrist pad and selected the cosmology feed. He disliked any heavy eye ware that took over the whole field of vision and the implants that sent the feed directly to the cerebral cortex. He preferred the tiny, detachable eye pads that attached just below the eye and came off easily.

"Mira is burning but its death will still take a million years. The cool, pulsating red giant, roughly 420 light-years away has now reached the diameter 700 times the Sun's. It is burning off its nuclear fuel and leaving behind a fifteen light-year-long tail, as it flows across the Milky Way towards its destruction. This will also be the eventual fate of the Sun. If you want to secure the future of your grandkids you need to buy an apartment on board 55 *Cancri* 1, the first ever star cruiser…"

He switched the feed off, stepped over the suitcases left on the platform, pulled out a can from his pocket, and inhaled pure oxygen. The air-conditioning on the platform did its best but failed to remove the smell of rot coming through the many invisible cracks in the floor, walls and ceiling.

"Take the exit four when you come to Russell Square."

"Subway four is closed due to emergency work on the semiconductor line."

"A café by the station serves full-flavoured Ethiopian espresso, your favourite mix. There will be three customers in the queue. That will make it thirty-six seconds in and out if you pre-order now."

The wrist pad's instructions often amounted to babysitting but occasionally it gave some useful information.

"I wouldn't do her if I was blind!" Nathan looked right and noticed a bunch of men in yellow overalls branded with the logo of the Martian Mining Corporation, sneering at some slightly overweight woman that passed by.

The workmen's rude sense of humour seemed galaxy-wide.

"Now that's some trimmed piece of ass!" a workman exclaimed.

A young woman, probably Indian, stood about ten feet right from him. She had a fair complexion, the light shade of brown that an upper caste Indian family looked for in a bride. She had Dark Peach E3As on her eyes, the trendiest model, nice visors, but not as striking to Nathan as her breasts whose piercings nearly broke the blue fabric of her body-hugger. The colours of her super-tight chameleon pants danced in the rhythm of her heartbeat. She adjusted the visor then glanced around as if she had sensed the stares.

Her eyes were like sliced kiwis.

Synthetic eyes cost a fortune.

She was a carefully constructed creature of the Underworld.

You could get synthetic eyes in any shape and form and connect them straight to virtual reality devices. They were illegal but the cops didn't really care about that kind of detail, not unless they were looking for an excuse to take someone off the streets.

She got in the carriage and sat next to an old man with a green tweed jacket, the kind he had seen at the Victoria & Albert Museum, in the department of men's fashion.

Nathan took the next carriage.

He sat down and started following the political debate on the Earth's first star cruiser from the Parliament of the Solar Nations in Geneva.

It played on the large screen above the passengers that sat opposite him. His ear amplifiers picked the sound which he adjusted with a slight sleight of his mind.

"We need to pull the plug on the project," the man he recognised as Iceland's Prime Minister said. "It's three hundred and thirty per cent over budget and five years overdue, and who knows, it might not be even able to take off. Why should we put the lives of over twenty-five thousand people in danger?"

"It is entirely safe, and the budget deficit will be covered through deals with the advertisers."

That was the voice of the US Secretary of State. "Besides, the future of the human race will depend on it."

"That's nonsense," the Icelander interrupted. "If we spent the budget to look after Earth we'd never need the ship!"

Nathan had heard the arguments for and against the star cruiser countless of times: when it took over thirty years to finish a job that was the biggest singular undertaking in Earth's history there was plenty of time to rehearse them. Nathan closed his eyes and reduced the sound levels so that the debate became hardly audible, merging into the background electric noise.

It was the loud bang or perhaps the abrupt deceleration of the train that shook him up. When he opened his eyes he saw a huge orange fireball hurling towards him. He held onto his seat and ducked, barely avoiding the force of the fireball that was preceded by scattered glass.

The train shrieked to a halt.

The carriage next to him was burning and the thick, black smoke was quickly spreading everywhere. It began to laminate itself onto the inside tissue of his lungs, forcing him to cough. Then, his ears popped open, and the vacuum of sound that had encapsulated him was gone.

He could hear screams and groans that sounded like coming from Hades. There was a smell of burning flesh.

Still, he couldn't see much because of the smoke, and the fact that even the emergency lights had gone dark.

Nathan switched the light of his wrist pad on. The communications were down and all the screen gave was frozen, electric light. Other passengers followed his lead, and soon, like fireflies, wrist pads began to gather around him. Together, they spread rays of light into the smoky darkness.

A woman lay on a pool of blood.

The men and women standing around looked panicked but

Nathan suspected that the panic had as much to do with the data link being down than the sight of devastation.

"Can you hear me?" Nathan knelt over the woman but got no response. He took hold of her wrist to check the data on the pad's screen. It was sending an emergency signal that was going nowhere.

Condition: critical. Pulse: 45.Time to death: 20min.

He looked at his own wrist pad again. The screen had frozen to the last transport update it had received. It showed that there were thirty-six passengers in the carriage. A dozen of them stood, the rest of them sat or lay on the floor amidst the broken glass, chunks of the furnishing and luggage.

How deep were they in the tunnel?

"We need to get everyone out fast."The speaker was a muscular African man in a business suit. The once-sleek suit was now torn, dirty and bloodied.

"Maybe we should just wait here, for the emergency services." Another man spoke, from the shadows.

"No, if we want to save lives. Some of the people here are badly hurt," the businessman said.

"The tracks might still be powered," a female voice protested. "We'll all get killed," she added.

"The power will go down automatically when there's an accident," Nathan said. "I remember seeing that in a safety broadcast," he said, for extra authority.

"In any case, we don't have to walk on the tracks," the businessman said. He went to the nearest exit door and tried to open it. It was jammed. He began kicking it, first gently then forcefully. The door gave in. Nathan heard a loud bang as the door hit the floor of the tunnel.

Nathan knelt over the woman who lay on the floor. He took a firm grip of her shoulders. Two men came to help him and, together, they carried her to the exit door. By now the physical action was sweeping away the panic and the helplessness from the faces of the passengers and they were amalgamating into a working team. The men jumped down and Nathan pushed the woman through the door.

Before letting her go Nathan glanced at her wrist pad once more.

Time to death: 10min.

Nathan stayed in the carriage, helping the injured out until the carriage was empty. Nobody even noticed that he stayed behind. He observed as the last of the men disappeared behind a curve in the tunnel, carrying the last injured. They were heading towards the Russell Square station as the way back had been blocked by a collapsed ceiling. The passengers in the back of the train would undoubtedly be trying to make it to King's Circle.

Behind the whisper of the burning flames someone or something was calling his name. It was nothing like an audible voice, but an awareness that forced its way into his consciousness.

He had discovered this awareness at the monastery, and it had never failed him.

The light from the wrist pad helped him to navigate through the carriage without stumbling onto anything. The upholstery was still burning. The black, toxic smoke forced its way deeper into the lungs, making breathing onerous. Nathan pulled an oxygen can from the pocket, inhaled pure oxygen for perhaps half a minute, put the can back into his pocket, and then kicked in what was left of the window glass that separated the two carriages. He climbed through the window and landed on something soft.

He stood still.

He could hear only the crackling and hissing of the many dark fires.

Behind the voice of the fire there was a solitary, feeble moan.

He stood there, in the dark, and waited.

Then he heard it again.

He began to walk towards the sound's direction, over the

broken seats, pieces of luggage, something soft, perhaps upholstery, or body parts.

He got to her.

Somehow he had known all along that it would be the Indian girl.

He scanned over her with his wrist pad. Some of the injuries were obvious; to start with, her left leg had been ripped away from below the knee.

She had been close to the epicentre but there must have been at least a few passengers between her and the explosion, protecting her from the full force of the blast. She was breathing but unconscious. He had a look at her wrist pad screen.

Time to death: 7min.

He had to get her out fast.

He took a firm grip of her, lifted her up and began to stumble over the debris. He pushed her through the broken window. At this point any further wounds from the glass hardly mattered. After he had pulled her out he sat there on the cold steel track, catching breath.

Time to death: 3 ½ min.

He got up and lifted her again on the shoulder. He rushed along the tunnel, as fast as he could, drawing strength from the moving shadows of the tunnel rats. Until now he had disbelieved the stories about the human skeletons with chew marks on them found in the tunnels, later on identified as missing workmen. He believed them now.The rats were at least three feet long, and, in his imagination, their teeth felt razor-sharp as they ripped his flesh.

After a while he saw a ray of light. He was getting close to Russell Square.

The platform was empty.

Somehow he managed to lift the girl up on the platform, climb up, and collapse next to her.

Time to death: 0min.

Her cheeks were lifeless, her body hugger darkened by the blood with patches of its fabric torn away, revealing the alien skin.

Outlawed in the Solar Nations, the alien skin made from synthetic materials had been invented in Japan, originally for all-night raves but it had run out of favour after dozens of people had died due to organ rejection. Some years later, the Japanese had developed DX-21 to counterattack the organ rejection but that had been too late to overturn the legislation. Anyone taking their daily dose of DX-21 would still meet a premature death, as the drug shortened the life span of the user with anything between ten and fifteen years.

Alien skin was popular with the sex workers of the Underworld; it could enhance and lengthen the pleasure with the massaging electric pulses that vibrated through the body, pulses that at worst or best could cause a permanent state of ecstasy.

Acquiring the alien skin wasn't that ecstatic: the surgical procedure started with the skinning of the patient.

He was still feeling dizzy when the blue rescue robots came to him. They were followed by the bright green first aiders. The robots put the girl on a stretcher, covered her face with a mask, and soon pipes went in and out of her body. The rescue robots descended on the track and headed into the tunnel.

He saw a human paramedic in the distance. She walked to him and knelt down.

"Are you alright?" she asked.

"I couldn't feel any better."

She fingered his wrist pad. All pads had an emergency override that gave immediate access to medical data.

"You are alright. Any idea how many people are still in the tunnel?"

"Don't you know?"

"All the data links are down."

"I doubt that there are any more survivors, not in the first two carriages." Nathan got up. "I have no idea what's going on in the other side."

It was then when he noticed that his clothes were soaked in blood.

"I'll need to get myself a new shirt."

"There's a makeshift first aid station in the hall. You should go there for screening."

Nathan's wrist pad reconnected to data networks when he reached the escalator and he could swear that the little rascal let out an audible sigh of relief.

The advertising screens went berserk. None of them took any heed of the privacy laws and in unison they began to push books on Egyptology, study courses in defunct African languages, 100% cotton khaki pants and augmented reality products, this time built around martial arts and Japanese meditation.

When he had come down the ads had been mostly about space trips, kinky sex products pushing the barriers of the advertising code, school uniforms, and ads for school uniforms as kinky sex products.

When he got to the station hall it was full to the point of bursting. He didn't want to waste any time there, so he headed toward the barricade of human policemen and robot cops in their dark navy vests and white shirts that were there to block the entrance to the station.

"Are you ok?" a human policeman that sported long dreadlocks asked him.

"I'm fine. There are a lot of people there that need more help than I."

"There's a dress machine around the corner. It can supply clothes for most tastes. You can always claim them on insurance."

The commuters took one look at his bloodied clothes and let him through.

"What happened?" somebody shouted from the crowd.

"I don't know. But I wouldn't wait for the next train."

The dress machine was around the corner, as the policeman had said. Nathan scanned his iris and the machine retrieved his preferences.

"Good morning, sir. You have lost some weight! How can I help?"

Nathan went for a pair of beige cotton trousers and a white linen shirt.

"They will be ready in three minutes, sir."

He waited until the clothes popped out. He didn't bother with the changing rooms but went to a nearby café instead. The barista let him use the restroom without asking any questions.

He must have seen the news.

Once in, he peeled off the blood-soiled clothes, stripping to the underpants. His chest was bruised and the skin on his shoulders red and broken but the injuries seemed only skin-deep. He splashed water on his face and midriff from the tap. He walked in one of the yellow cubicles, sat on the toilet cover and closed the door.

The aftershock hit him. He sat there, sweated heavily, the cool air from the ventilation system not breezy enough to dry the skin.

He had been staring, unfocused, at the floor tiles for quite a while when he noticed the bloodstains on his shoes.

He got out of the cubicle, went to the sink, removed the shoes and rinsed the bloodstains away.

3.

It took Nathan few minutes to walk back to Russell Square. Greater London covered over 3,500 square miles of land but similar industries, business areas and organisations tended to cluster together—he was only a short walking distance from London's many universities, the Old British Library and the British Museum.

He had tried to call Jack to let him know that he was running late but he hadn't been able to get through. The data lines flicked on and off haphazardly. The explosion must have had disrupted a major communication line.

The streets were in chaos as the underground had been shut down completely and the bright red overground shuttles and black cabs were bursting with passengers. Many had given up waiting and walked.

The School of African Studies was a brown-brick, four-storey building located in the campus of London University. Its round, ugly façade stood out in the even uglier building complex that had been built in the Modernist era. No refurbishment project had been able to conceal the monstrous mistakes of its original architects. Most of the tall Modernist blocks that had disfigured the city's skyline had been demolished soon after the Do-Muzude, as they had become a haven for rats, insects, and all sorts of animals mankind had spent half of its history trying to exterminate.

The campus was one of the rare Modernist constructions left in the city. It was almost beautiful in its ugliness.

The school ran one or two galaxy-class research projects but had always suffered from lack of funding. The government had nothing to give, and when it came to private investors, there wasn't much money for them to make from the Outworld's past.

Nathan discovered at the reception that Jack had arrived only five minutes earlier.

He took the lift to the fourth floor.

Jack Tomhalt, the Head of the Department of Study of Religion relaxed on his large black leather chair behind the desk that was as vast and unpredictable as Sahara. Heaps of dusty books and paper reports formed hazardous dunes where even a slight move of hand could trigger a book slide that would make everything come down. The religious artefacts bursting out of the cramped shelves on the wall were from all around the solar system.

Jack lit up when he saw Nathan but he didn't waste any time on greetings.

"See this!"

He picked a small piece of rock from the desk.

"It was found in the Ophir Chasma in the Valles Marineris, a huge canyon system in Mars. Many archaeologists think that it was part of an extra-terrestrial altar."

He threw the rock at Nathan who barely managed to catch it.

The rock felt heavy and smooth. It looked as if it were pure, refined iron.

"Why's that?"

"I don't know. There is nothing about that rock that stands out. But according to some in the Faculty of Alien Religions in Oxford, the fact that there is nothing noteworthy about it is the very evidence that it has been manufactured by some alien technology and proves that the alien species inhabiting the Red Planet some millions of years ago had a radically different way to build religious artefacts than we do."

Nathan smiled. Jack was a known for his scepticism regarding extra-terrestrial religions, but this time, he might have had a point.

"That rock and its kind are worth millions for them. Based on one or two samples, the Faculty of Alien Religions has just been granted one and a half billion yuan grant to explore the origins of Martian religions. That's only hundred times our annual budget!"

Nathan placed the stone on the glass table by the sofa and sat down.

"How did you get that stone?" he asked.

"The government is required to consult specialists before giving any grants of that size. That doesn't mean that they care about my opinion but they can claim that they have talked to all camps."

"I've also spent time with some stones."

"What kind of stones?" Jack asked. "Is there any money in them?"

"We dug around thirty megalithic alignments which all seem to have astrological significance. Also, we found a sun calendar."

"I'm listening."

"It seems that the stone circles of Nabta Playa are in fact at least thousand years older than any circles in Britain. Their builders knew astrology at least a millennium before the Sumerians. They are the oldest structure built with astronomical understanding known to man."

"Could it be an Egyptian outpost?"

"Not quite."

Nathan sipped water from the glass that a minuscule robot waiter had just served.

"The fossilised remains of people buried there and the way they were buried proves conclusively that the builders were sub-Saharan black Africans."

Jack was rocking in his chair.

That was always a sign that he was deep in thought.

"Is that result based on carbon dating?"

"Yes. The dating has also been confirmed by two independent labs. They are at least six thousand years old, maybe even six thousand and five hundred. They are the second oldest religious constructions that we know of."

"The first solid structure that was erected on Eris was a stone circle. What a waste of resources! An uninhabitable planet, barely a hundred AU from the Sun, and the first thing they do is to build a stone circle." Jack started his customary rant at the Order. "Who knows, a druid might pass by once every thousand years. That money would have funded our university for the next five hundred years."

Jack stopped rocking the chair and looked at Nathan straight in the eye.

"You know well that around forty-five per cent of Oxford's funding comes from the Order. It won't be looking at your project kindly."

"That's why I'm here. The funding for further work has just been withdrawn, with an immediate effect."

Jack glanced at the old Egyptian sun clock, placed on a miniature globe that orbited a slightly larger sun which powered it with its light.

"I must go now."

Jack got up and picked his briefcase.

"Be careful. You know that the Order's machinery can be pretty brutal when they start a fight."

"I'm not starting a fight."

"The Order isn't interested in your motivations, only in what you do. You should know that."

They were out and within seconds, Nathan was already sweating.

"Sure you don't want a lift?" Jack asked.

"I'll be fine."

"The chauffeur can drop you anywhere, after it has taken me to my meeting. The public transport will be disrupted until the evening. It will be hard to get around."

"I'm not exactly sure where I'll go next."

The long black hoverer's side door opened.

"Good morning, the lord of the Philistines." The chauffeur was a robot but spoke with a cheerful female voice, and in Akkadian, the language of the ancient Assyrians. "Where do you want to go, my lord?"

To steal the hoverer you would have to be a rather exceptional thief.

"11 Downing Street." Jack sat down on the back seat but kept on talking through the open window.

"I can help you with funding if you're ready to stay in London for a series of lectures. That is, as long as you are willing to tolerate some publicity."

Nathan watched as Jack's hoverer took off and floated into the slow traffic.

A lecture series! What difference could some esoteric lecture series in one of the world's most underfunded academic institute make? The reality was that Jack's impressive address book had very little to do with his job and a lot more with his family. No one in the world really cared about the School of African Studies, only Jack, and a few deluded students who thought that studying the African past could possibly sound more fashionable than the igloo studies.

4.

Above surface, London was all glitter and glitz but under the street level the remnant of the old city was rotting away. Long before the Do-Muzude the city had begun to grow downwards, and eventually the office blocks had reached the depth of half a mile with the housing complexes spiralling hundreds of miles away from the city. At the height of the underground building movement over ten million people had lived under the city, and another twenty million had commuted there to work. The motivation for building the underground city had been to preserve what was left of the island's green space. Every inch had mattered. The green belt around London had consisted largely of vast stretches of fields for super-crops with areas of vacuum-sealed greenhouses that produced GM free organic crops for the wealthy littered in between, pretty much the same way than today.

Fifty-four years ago over two thirds of the underground population had drowned as the first mega-tsunami had broken the unbreakable floodgates. It had been followed by others, as the world's weather system underwent a rapid, unexpected change. For three years, the once-friendly oceans had become mankind's worst enemy.

After the Do-Muzude—the word came from Japanese and meant 'doomsday'—the rabbis, gurus, druids, self-declared prophets and their scientific equivalents had all tried to demonstrate that their sacred texts had foreseen the destruction. Comparatively, London had fared well. Of the existing nations, the destruction had hit Japan the hardest with Tokyo and Kyoto, its two largest cities, reduced to rubbles. It had hit the Netherlands even harder but then, it was no more. The Dutch had been able to evacuate most of the people to France and Switzerland during one of the world history's best organised projects of exile, so they had remained as people, and become the most vocal campaigners for space colonisation.

Perhaps one day there would be a planet called the New Dutchland.

Japan's Prime Minister had coined the name for the series of disasters by shouting 'Do-muzude!' and plunging into his sword in the middle of a live news conference.

After the third mega-tsunami had come a medieval-style plague triggered by the new variation of Variola major, the smallpox virus that had escaped a Shanghai bio-development lab whose walls had been cracked by the waves.

As a newly created archipelago, London had been saved from the devastating impact of the virus, but not from many lesser evils.

Around four hundred million body bags later the antidote had been developed. The fourth mega-tsunami had shaken the Arctic, breaking around forty-five per cent of its ice mass. This had raised the sea levels by thirty feet, enough to push Europe's shoreline inland by twenty-five miles and sink the early beginnings of New Holland. Miraculously, the continent of Africa, or the Outworld, had been saved from much of these disasters. Apart from losing a few coastal cities such as Cape Town the poverty-stricken continent had continued its shabby existence.

America had been less lucky but it had been the coastline cities that had been devastated whilst life had continued as normal in Utah, apart from the millions of refugees.

The locals said that weather in Utah was a lot better than it used to be.

In London, the floodwaters had stayed for two and half years, poisoning the groundwater for gods knew how long, destroyed over half of the surface city, and most of the underground infrastructure, creating the notorious Underworld, the world of the others.

That was where the Indian girl had come from. Nobody owned the Underworld, so the housing there came rent-free, but you were better off sleeping with a weapon next to you, as you could never know who or what could crash through your bedroom wall. It was the stench of the Underworld that seeped through the pores of the city, reaching the nostrils of the pedestrians, especially on a hot day.

Most Underworlders that could afford it had gone through the genetic treatment that let them control their sense of smell at will; others had got rid of their sense of it altogether.

He walked down the street to the park in Russell Square and Café Galactica by the gigantic water fountain to escape the heat. Galactica's beans were harvested from the fields that orbited at the height of two hundred and fifty miles from Earth—growing in nearly zero gee. The perfect control over the exposure to the Sun gave them their unique nutty flavour. As there were no harmful insects, viruses or bacteria in their ecosystem the farmers had no need for pesticides and the beans were advertised as 'vacuum packed space beans', free of the pollution and dirt so omnipresent on Earth.

The café was nearly full but he found an empty chair. Seconds later, a lanky robot waiter came to take an order. Nathan asked for a frosted Americano with plenty of ice and fixed his eyes on the news screen.

All sorts of AllNet media was already bustling at King's Circle. The entrance to the underground station remained blocked by a barricade of robot cops.

"At 8.55am this morning, a carriage departing from King's Circle exploded inside the Northern line's southbound tunnel."

The young reporter struggled to conceal the undertone of excitement.

It was a bad day for London but an excellent news day.

"The cause is still unknown. What we do know is that there have been many casualties."

Nathan waited until the news program returned to the BBC studios and the chubby and bald news anchor Alan Midget, one of the best paid people in the news business.

"The trains and shuttles travelling in and out of the capital are suspended. We advise you to avoid any travel until we know more."

What followed was a mixture of facts, buzz, conjectures and outright fiction. It took another fifteen minutes before Alan said anything actually newsworthy.

"The Metropolitan Police has now confirmed that the explosion was caused by a bomb."

The café quietened and everyone turned to the screens.

"The exact number of casualties is still unclear. The emergency services are still working their way through the rubble," Alan continued. "James Lumbdon, a City banker at Mercurial Securities was caught in the explosion."

James was your regular City type, in his late thirties, unless he popped anti-ageing pills. He had the early beginnings of a gut. His suit was torn and dirty, and the formerly white shirt had been smeared by the tunnel dust.

"What happened?"

"It was like any other mornings." He scrubbed his shirt, trying to clean it in vain as he spoke. The dirt just spread and made the smudges even more visible.

"There was a huge explosion, and then came a scorching-hot fireball. It all went pitch black. There was a lot of screaming."

"What did you do?"

"We got some light from the wrist pads, broke through an exit and then got everyone out."

"So no one was left behind?"

"We searched through the exploded carriage. No one was left alive."

"That was brave."

"Anyone would have done the same."

"Thank you." Alan turned to camera. "This morning, James, a Londoner, was on his way to work when he was caught up in the explosion. He put his life in danger to save others. He might not call himself a hero but he is one. He epitomises our ability to defeat terrorism. We will shortly be talking to him again but now we will hear from John Nootstill, the nation's leading terrorism expert."

He turned to the fat, middle-aged man who had materialised next to him.

"John, what's your view?"

"It is clear that an explosive device blew up in the carriage number two."

An animation of the explosion in the train filled the screen.

"The bomb was powerful but crude."

"How do you know that it was a bomb?"

"With a bomb, the explosive pressure imparts a high velocity to the fragments of its casing. The fragments tear flesh more severely than bullets, as their flight pattern is unstable and the pieces penetrate flesh at fast speed but along a tumbling path. The injuries that we have seen so far indicate that this is the case. Also, there is the blast wave."

"What is that?"

John resembled an about-to-retire primary school teacher forced to explain the same things to yet another lot of six-year-olds.

"An explosion is always followed by a blast wave. It has two components. First, a positive pressure followed by a negative phase, then a mass movement of air. Injuries come mainly from the initial shock wave but are aggravated by the sub-atmospheric negative phase. The positive pressure phase of the blast wave lasts only a few milliseconds but close to an explosion it may be devastating. Like sound waves, the blast pressure waves flow over and around an obstruction and affect anyone sheltering behind a wall. The negative phase of a pressure wave is of less amplitude but lasts longer than the positive phase. A mass movement of air results from the rapidly expanding gases at the heart of an explosion which displace air at high velocity. This mass movement of air causes a blast wind which may result in total disintegration of the body and, at lesser levels, traumatic amputation."

"That sounds serious."

"The explosive blast causes fragmentation of tissues. Ear drums, the air sacs in the lung and the gas-filled intestinal organs, both structures with fluid and air interfaces, are particularly susceptible to damage by blast waves."

"How fatal is that?"

"Over forty per cent of the people hit by the blast wave will die of organ failure, unless they get immediate medical help."

"How many people would have died?"

Café Galactica was now perfectly quiet, apart from the news story blasting from the speakers.

"Hundreds would have suffered minor injuries, many simply due to the abrupt stop. Close to the epicentre of the explosion—and that would include the whole exploded carriage—the fatality rate would have been nearly hundred per cent."

"Who could be behind this terrorist act?"

"There are many possibilities. It could be a separatist group from the Underworld, a revenge attack from the Outworld, animal rights activists, or any of the groups opposing the annexation of the rest of the solar system to the Solar Nations."

Nathan had heard enough. He got up and left the café.

5.

After three days of bombardment from the fifteen mortars that had been dragged from the ship with the cost of the lives of twenty-one mules and two soldiers—the soldiers had been crushed under a falling mortar—the officers finally considered it safe to advance to the mountain fortress of Maqdala.

There was no resistance.

The hostages, locked in a dungeon, were the only people alive, hungry and thirsty but unharmed. The only other living creatures they encountered were the vultures feeding on the remains of the once great Abyssinian army.

The Emperor Tewodoros lay on the ground with a single bullet hole in the forehead and maggots crawling over his body.

He was buried in a simple, unmarked tomb, seven feet deep.

According to an Ethiopian legend he would be resurrected on the third day.

After three days, he still lay there. Seven feet deep.

Yet, after thirty-one years of ruling, raping, and butchering his people they still paid him respect. It was as if their god had died; an ill-tempered and unpredictable one perhaps, but a god nevertheless.

The release of the hostages became an anti-climax after the soldiers realised that the sole reason behind their deployment and months-long journey was to set a group of druid missionaries free.

The disappointment was soon forgotten when a soldier discovered the Emperor's wine cellar. It took the army three hours to drag two thousand barrels of wine out, two hours to distribute them and fifteen minutes to drink it all, a fine example of the skill and effectiveness of the British army.

Richard hadn't travelled this far to get drunk; he'd had enough wine at home. He had come for the Emperor's books.

Captain Eric Barratt, slightly too choppy and round-faced for a soldier but one regardless, guided Richard to the entrance of the library. His face was red from wine, nearly as red as his officer's jacket.

"That's what you came looking for," he slurred. "Don't see why but there it is! There is plenty of gold and jewellery for the rest of us." He pulled a cigar out of his breast pocket, lit it with a match, and grinned. He had tarred, yellow smoker's teeth.

"I'll somehow steal the golden throne. It will go missing between leaving Ethiopia and arriving in London. Hell, what do I care about what you want! There'll be one less man splitting the pot. Can you believe it? The general has already allocated half of the ransom to the British Museum! I bet none of it will ever make it there."

Richard was hardly listening. He opened the wooden door that led to the library.

"If those monks were right, you will never be able to read them," Eric said. "Nobody will."

"They didn't have the aid of modern linguistics. Please pass me the matches."

Eric tossed the matchbox to Richard. He lit a match and looked in.

There was very little draft and the match burnt brightly. The first thing he saw was a golden candle stand with candlesticks. He lit a candle before the match burnt out. Then he took the candle and lit the rest of the candles.

"Can you believe they have a Menorah here?"

"What's that?" Eric asked.

"It's a Jewish candle stand."

"What have they got to do with the Jews?"

"The Ethiopians believe they are a lost tribe of Israel."

His eyes began to adjust to the dim light. The library was much larger than he could have ever imagined.

"There are thousands of parchments, books and rolls!"

There was line after line of shelves, filled with ancient texts. Even Eric, who had followed him in, seemed impressed.

"You're not taking all of them to London!"

"Relax. There'll be plenty of mules left for your gold."

Two weeks later, when the army left Magdala, twenty-three of the over three hundred mules had been loaded with books, scrolls and parchments, each of them carefully packed by Richard who knew already that he would be spending the rest of his life in attempting to decipher them.

That he would do, often infuriating his wife by staying at the British Library long after the rest of the staff had gone home. Often when he woke up in the morning he found himself slumped over his desk in the office.

6.

It took Nathan four and a half hours to make it to Lola's apartment. Walking seemed the only option with overground shuttles hopelessly overcrowded, the electromagnetic tracks struggling to keep them afloat, and the whole underground system shut down. He tried to hail a taxi but they were all full. The queue at the taxi ranks extended around the corner wherever he went.

The sunshine was scorching, making the streets into a fiery furnace, so he popped into every air-conditioned shop and shopping mall he could find on the way.

He called Lola in the office to warn her that he was coming but heard that she was out, meeting with clients. He got no contact with her wrist pad. Born in the Outworld, she was comfortable being offline, unlike the rest of the population that would have had to resort to tranquillisers to achieve that kind of feat.

She wasn't the only one, although complete abstinence was rare and impossible if you wanted to work or study. One Buddhist sect asked its members to abstain from wrist pads and then there were the criminals and fugitives that got rid of theirs but then got a hacked one from the Underworld, one that came with a false identity. Everybody else kept their wrist pads on at all times, muting them for the duration of religious liturgies such as weddings, funerals and blessings for robots at best. For most people wrist pads were like oxygen, like water.

The outdated models were cleaned up, recycled and sold to the Outworld. He had seen the Bedouins and Berbers in Sahara finding their way across the rapidly shifting dunes with their help, making the ancient skills of navigation passed on by fathers to sons redundant.

Some scientists warned about their negative effects and said that the way they smoothed off the rough edges of human experience and reduced the need for conscious thinking would in the long term lead to the shrinking and eventual disappearing of the human brain.

Hardly anyone listened to them.

Everyone had a wrist pad within five minutes of their birth.

Nathan had been twenty-three and in Japan when he had taken his wrist pad off for the first time ever.The withdrawal symptoms had begun with deep-level anxiety, the trembling of hands and feet, and cold sweat. His nerves and brain were bursting, as they sought for their regular feed. Without the encouragement and help from the monks at the temple he would never have been able to pull through. After three days the tidal pain had begun to subside and clear thoughts had begun to stream through his mind.

They felt painful and he had to push them out as if giving birth but they had a strange vibrancy and reality about them which he had never experienced before.

His mind felt like an alien planet, terrifying and wonderful. Formulating a thought had never been harder but every thought came with an intensity of a laser ray, bringing clarity and light. They lit up the alleyways that had been dark, bringing shadows to pitch-black.

He had wrapped the pad around his wrist again a month later. It had morphed itself into his body as if it had never been separated from him. He kept it on most the time, although he was now slightly alarmed of its ability to bring unnatural ease into his thoughts.

He took the wrist pad off most nights, even when his dreams often became nightmares.

He walked to Charing Cross Road and popped into Foyles, a bookstore in the moulded centre of the city. Somehow it had managed to stay open, even when there never seemed to be any customers. Once upon a time, the whole street had been occupied by the bookstores, but only Foyles had withstood the strangulating effect of new technologies.

He picked books from the dirt-stained mahogany shelves at whim and with no plan, caressing the fingerprints, grease, and coffee stains. It took him an hour and a half to make it the Department of the Outworld History.

It was a whole floor filled with ancient books and manuscripts, some in mint condition, others barely readable. The history of Outworld had never been a popular subject, not even before the Solar Nations had shut Africa from the rest of the world and named it 'Outworld'.

As usual, the department was empty of people. He looked around until he found the books that focused on the history of Aksum, the ancient Ethiopian kingdom. This part of the bookstore was disconnected from the AllNet; no cataloguing had ever taken place.

He chose two books. They were protected by transparent plastics, rare hardbacks, originally printed only in hundreds. Their pages were white, bleached paper, and they were in mint condition. He paid for them, a substantial amount, and left, the books packed in a brown paper bag.

He walked through Chinatown, one of the entry points to the Underworld. It was looked after by Triads and the cops left them to run their businesses, as long as the body count remained low. All around there were tables selling bootlegged wrist pads, and the shop windows mostly displayed robots performing acrobatic sex simulations.

Chinatown was notorious for fake-brand household robots

shipped from low-cost manufacturing countries such as Germany. They tended to break down quickly but if you went back to reclaim your money you'd probably find out that the shop you bought the robot from had disappeared.

He bought some Chinese dumplings from a market stall, then headed to Oxford Street only to discover that the long shopping street had become virtually un-passable. The crowds of pedestrians spilled onto the street, making the voyage of the many taxis and shuttles bumpy as their automated crash-prevention systems tried to deal with the pedestrians that completely ignored them. He followed a parallel street with less traffic and walked on the shadowy side to avoid the sun.

The subway under Hyde Park was air-conditioned and by the time he neared Kensington High Street in the other side of the park he felt cool and fresh, only the residual scent of musk reminding him of sweat. He went in to an off-license and picked a bottle of Mason Sauvignon Blanc, bottled in Napa Valley and then walked to the cricket ground in Holland Park. He sat there under a palm tree and watched kids playing with robot pets and eating ice creams. He stayed there until 5.45pm, playing the events of the day in his mind.

Nathan didn't believe in gods but he prayed that the Indian girl he had dragged out of the train wreck would make it.

Lola's apartment was situated at the edge of Holland Park, on the third floor of a Victorian townhouse, a building whose exterior had changed very little in the last three hundred years, albeit it had taken a lot of effort to maintain the appearance of changelessness.

It had been well over a year since he had seen Lola the last time.

He climbed the stairs up and pressed the front door bell. There was no response.

It was 6.15pm, forty-five minutes after her work shift normally ended.

He sat on the stairs for half an hour, until finally a pink scooter hovered past him, slowed down and parked by the pavement.

A pink helmet, grey pinstripe dress suit and shiny, black leather boots.

Lola took her helmet off which liberated her afro that returned to its perfect shape.

Then she saw him.

"That's some mighty hairspray," he said. "And you're moving up in the galaxy! Pink scooters like that don't come cheap!"

"Oh, the Lamborghini! I got it with the bonus."

He gave her a hug. Her cheeks were still burning from the ride. They smelled of roses, violet, jasmine, lily, orchid and honey. He knew the list as they were the ingredients of her favourite perfume.

"You need a shower," she said.

"I don't disagree. It's hot like hell."

Lola looked at him, from head to toe, and flashed her white, pearly teeth.

"You'll not be able to get out of London tonight. The city hoppers are all still out of use, until they scan all of them. And the tracks. You can stay with me for the night."

"It crossed my mind."

The door scanner read her iris and the door slid open.

"Please give Nathan McKinley a guest pass," she instructed the security system.

"Yes, madam," the response came with a friendly female voice. He followed her up the stairs, the floor planks shrieking under their weight.

"The flooring was here well before the Do-Muzude," she said.

Like most London apartments, Lola's was fairly small. It consisted of a small reception room, a slightly larger bedroom, bathroom, kitchen and a long corridor that united everything. He went to the bathroom, took off his clothes, put them in the washing machine and had a shower.

The clothes were waiting for him, dried and ironed when he came out of the shower cubicle.

Lola was cooking. He sat down by the vast oak table that dominated the kitchen and let his eyes feast on her. Their relationship had always officially been strictly platonic but that didn't mean it couldn't have had some sensual undertones.

She had slipped into a yellow, flowery dress that embraced her five foot eight tall body. It was one of those pieces that revealed through concealment. Her skin was a rare shade of dark mahogany. She had always loved dancing, and even now when cooking, her body swang softly. She had high eyebrows and cheekbones, large brown eyes and full lips.

A beautiful woman.

"What?" she asked, sensing his eyes on her body.

"Nothing."

He moved his eyes on to the 3D holograph on the wall, depicting an African warrior.

"It has been a while since we met. My backside is still sore from the injections I had to take before they let me back to England. When I called your workplace I heard that you got promoted."

"I brought in the exclusive advertising contract for 55 *Cancri 1*."

"That star cruiser?"

"Or three and a half million square feet of unsold advertising space. I'll be up there most of the next week, mapping the spots."

"Don't get stuck. The voyage will take forty-five years."

The supper was Chinese dumplings served with plantains and Nigerian curry, all flushed down with the bottle of wine he had brought with the dumplings.

They laughed about past times, gossiped about the misadventures of common friends, and watched an ancient Clint Eastwood flat film. Nathan fell asleep before it ended. When he woke up, she was in her pyjamas, watching a documentary.

"That's the ship," she said. A gigantic star cruiser orbited Earth, at the height of three hundred miles. "It is so large that they aren't able to manufacture engines powerful enough to produce the acceleration force to leave the Earth's gravitational field. That's why it's built in space."

"What will happen when it gets there? How will they stop it?"

"They won't. There will be five hundred evacuation ships leaving the star cruiser. It will continue its trajectory, and turn into space junk. Or get sucked into a black hole. It isn't economical to stop it completely."

Nathan watched as a large jump ship approached the star cruiser. It looked like a mosquito landing on an elephant.

"Take some pictures of Mother Earth when you get there."

7.

When he woke up the room was dark. The red digits of the wall clock showed that the time was 6.09am. Lola must have covered him with a blanket after he had fallen asleep as he didn't remember having one. She had gone to sleep in her bedroom.

He got up to open the curtains. He opened the window and breathed in the cool air from the outside.

It still smelled fresh.

In a few hours' time the street would be as hot as a frying pan.

He had met Lola for the first time at the Oxford University's Gentlemen's Chess Club.

In truth, it hadn't been much of a chess club; chess was played there, but it was a cover story for smoking Cuban cigars which had been banned in the Solar Nations for the last forty-eight years.

Smoking cigarettes was illegal; smoking Cuban cigars was even more so because of some ancient trade disagreements between Cuba and one of the largest Solar Nations, the United States of America.

It was also unlawful to discriminate against women but the law students that were members of the gentlemen's club had managed to keep its name through appealing to tradition, and making a claim that the word 'gentleman' didn't discriminate against women but in fact referred to men as the 'gentler' sex, and that the name was in fact slightly derogatory to men, but that they could live with that.

So, the club was unisex by law but male in practice. The doors were kept wide open for any female to walk in. No one ever did.

Most female students headed to the rugby ground populated by handsome athletes in tight shorts rather than ventured into the club's smoky rooms.

It had been a sleepy afternoon, the time after Sunday roast when all your blood is still busy dealing with a nutrition overdose. Nathan dozed off in a dark purple leather chair. Michael sat next to him, smoking a cigar. When he leant forward he looked like an owl, albeit a starved one, as his large brown eyes, further magnified by his very old-fashioned spectacles, gleamed through the smoke.

"Kasparov 213.3 is simply unbeatable," Michael said. "It will have defeated you even before you start the game. It knows all the possible moves and can calculate every possible combination simultaneously. Mikhail Prostov did get a stalemate once but that was with the help of his wrist pad. It was linked to the collective minds of over ten thousand of the solar system's best ranked players. The story is he would have lost had it not been for Alex Birnsby, who worked at a Martian research station at the time."

Michael loved his chess stories but not everyone did. Even Nathan was only feigning interest. "With the delay in communications due to the distance to Mars, Alex was able to pre-test the moves by playing against another copy of the program, and without losing any time. Kasparov 213.3 was really playing against itself. The lesson is that it can't be beaten."

"Yes it can."

Who was that?

Nathan turned around and saw a slender black girl with braided hair. His first impression of her was that there was a woman who knew what she wanted, an impression that had by and large withstood the test of time.

"And who are you?" Michael asked, the tone of his voice somewhere between sneer and incomprehension.

"I am Lola."

"How would you beat Kasparov 213.3?"

"By pulling the plug. The battery will run out."

She had beautiful eyes, full of spark, humour and tenderness, and since then her slim body had filled up nicely.

She had been new in town and hadn't known her way around, so he had walked her home. They had spent a lot of time together. Then she had vanished without even leaving a message. Her roommate had told him she had gone home in the Outworld to deal with some family business.

She had returned a year later. She didn't talk much about her experiences back in the Yoruba Land but he could detect newfound sadness and occasional fear in her eyes. She looked as young as before but her soul had aged. Through her eyes, you could occassionally peek into a momentary emptiness.

She never told him, he never asked. Still, he always made her smile.

He sat on the floor, took a Lotus position and fixed his eyes on the singular blue thread in the beige carpet. He focused on it until his sight started to blur.

Mind is like a river; it never empties itself.

It can't.

The only way to find peace is to step on a rock and watch it stream by.

"Get up! The breakfast is ready." Lola's voice hammered its way into his consciousness. "Had I foreseen this, I'd have had the carpet cleaned earlier. You can't find any enlightenment in that carpet. Only dirt. And Robin is about to take it away."

An ellipse-shaped, dachshund-sized robot circled in the doorway, looking agitated.

It eyeballed him with its laser beam eyes, seemingly irritated about the disruption in its cleaning schedule.

"Ready in five minutes!" he said, trying to keep his eyes fixed on the thread.

He caught a reflection of her in the mirror. It was really a double reflection, a reflection of a reflection, a mirror image in a mirror.

For a brief moment he was certain that Lola wore nothing else but something that resembled a lacy, red bra.

The reflection vanished.

According to Buddha, man is like a cart made of five aggregates: matter, sensation, perception, mental formations and consciousness. Behind them rolls the Wheel of Life, spinning an illusion of personhood around man and tying him into millions of rebirths. The Wheel of Life is fuelled by man's lusts and desires that delude him to believe in the illusion of individual existence.

Right now, his wheel of life was spinning out of control.

Ten minutes later he was by the oak table, enjoying porridge made from freshly ground seeds with strawberries that looked like they had been picked the same morning.

"These are from the orbital fields," Lola said.

"There are regions in the Outworld that don't get sunshine because of the fields," Nathan said. Lola's smile froze.

"I can't eat them now," she said, dropping a half-eaten strawberry back on the plate.

"Sorry. I didn't mean to wreck your appetite."

"Not your fault. The city hoppers are back working."

"Great. I'll be travelling back to Oxford tonight. But I'll be back in London next week."

"You can always come to sleep on the sofa. I'll be back from 55 *Cancri 1* on Thursday evening." She looked at her wrist pad.

"I'm running late," she said. She got up, gave him a hasty hug, and rushed out of the door. It was amazing how swiftly she could switch on her work mode.

He finished the porridge and the strawberries without haste. He had stopped letting politics affect his culinary enjoyment long ago, otherwise he would have been unable to eat anything. It seemed nearly impossible to discern between good and evil when it came to the solar economy. Good intentions often had evil consequences and sometimes, one man's blind greed inadvertently brought prosperity to a nation. The web of causes and effects seemed far too complex for a singular man to untie.

Lola's kitchen robot came and served him some coffee and toast. After finishing the breakfast he went to the living room. There were many Nigerian artefacts on the mantelpiece. He touched an ivory cup and let his fingers slide over its circular base that had rows of carved animal figures. Lola was a Yoruba princess, from one of the largest Nigerian tribes. He took an *udamalore* from the wall. It was an ivory ceremonial sword that the most high-ranking tribal chiefs wore on the hip.

He made a few plunging strikes with it.

The swords could occasionally be bought at antique markets but this sword must have had some personal connection to Lola. Its handle had the form of a stretched-necked human head with heavy-lidded eyes, full lips, and braids. Its curved blade was divided in two parts—close to the handle there was a section decorated with knot patterns. The upper section depicted a chief in a ceremonial dress, wearing a sword. The chief held a bird in the left hand and a sword in the right. The upraised sword was an *uda*, the sword used for defence. Nathan was familiar enough with the Yoruba culture to know that the bird referred to the spiritual powers of the old Yoruba women whose prayers were seen to carry a special protective shield. These emblems combined to generate an image of a ruler who was physically and spiritually ready to meet whatever challenges the tribe or the village would face.

He put the sword back on the wall and picked a cylindrical ivory bracelet that was on the mantelpiece. Its engravings depicted two figures that were dressed as rulers and other figures including attendants. Some smoked a pipe, others blew a flute;

there were crocodiles and warriors on horseback, a warrior with a severed head and bound captives. He had seen a similar one in the British Museum.

It was a very rare piece of jewellery that was traditionally worn only by high-ranking Yoruba royals.

There was a foot-long pink cylinder on the coffee table, the kind most people used to access their personal recordings. Nathan willed it on.

It was a family album, and as it began to project two-dimensionally on the wall he saw that the records had been organised chronologically. They started from childhood. For a second he felt a pinch of guilt for breaching her privacy but then he reckoned that the cylinder wouldn't be there if it was meant to be concealed from visitors.

She had been a choppy baby.

Lola had been raised in the Outworld but when she was twelve her family had moved to Edinburgh where her Scottish accent came from. Most of the footage had been shot by robots. He realised that the tiny robot cinematographers had even captured him at a party at Lola's place. He skipped that and looked for a time when Lola had been in Nigeria.

He saw a thumbnail of Lola in a golden-coloured Yoruba headpiece, wrap skirt, and a shawl. He chose that. It was a traditional tribal dress, and she stood next to a middle-aged Yoruba man in slacks, shirt, long jacket and a rounded box-like hat. The Yoruba tribe liked to dress to any occasion, but this one seemed extra-special. He chose the 3D view and stepped into the footage so that he could get a 360° view.

It was a wedding party.

Women in their colourful dresses knelt down while the men prostrated themselves on the floor in front of their future in-laws. That would be a long ceremony, he knew, so he jumped to the actual engagement, which consisted of the exchange of rings and the unveiling of the bride. The groom was the middle-aged

Yoruba man he had seen in the introduction of the recording. The bride's face was veiled but Nathan knew that it would be Lola even before she removed the veil.

She never told him that she had got married. She had never even mentioned a husband.

It all seemed like an arranged marriage gone awry. He stopped the recording and turned his attention to the news, playing on the screen. He flicked through the channels until he found *Galactic News*.

"In total, thirty-eight passengers died in the explosion," the reporter said. She stood in front of a truck that was offloading clearing robots in front of the King's Circle underground station. "Hundreds have been inflicted with horrendous injuries. The post-explosion investigation has already confirmed what the experts suspected—that the explosion was caused by a bomb in the carriage number two. The traces from the explosive device resemble the ones that the Solar Anti-Colonization Group used over twenty years ago." Droplets of sweat rolled down her cheeks and forehead.

The portable cooling unit stationed behind her was failing to remove the heat.

"One of the dead is Guinevere. She was twenty-seven. She was the daughter of Edward McKinley. He is our Minister of Defence."

The broadcast transferred to the news studio.

"Edward is currently at the Cabinet's crisis meeting but his brother and Guinevere's uncle, the chief druid Dr Michael McKinley, is here with us."

Next to the host, a lean, middle-aged man in a beige linen suit sat the leader of the Order. At sixty-seven, he still looked handsome and fit. His light tan contrasted with his white hair and long beard.

"This is a time for deep grief," he said, clearing his throat. "It is the assurance of the afterlife that gives us the strength to carry on." The chief druid's grief was never merely personal but it had to accommodate the differing views of the many factions of the Order on the afterlife.

"What is the Order doing to help the people who have lost their loved ones?" the host asked.

"We are here to remind that death isn't the end. And after all, that's the greatest thing we can ever do. We will have a vigil at Trafalgar Square starting from 8pm tonight."

Nathan switched the screen off, packed his things and headed to the door.

It had been three years since he'd seen Dad.

A face-to-face meeting with him had just become unavoidable.

8.

Nathan hailed a taxi from Holland Park Avenue and began the infuriatingly slow hovering toward Hampstead. In most of London there were only three lanes, the lowest for 10mph or under, the middle lane for speeds under 25mph, and the top lane for speeds up to 40mph. The top speeds were theoretical, as due to the congestion it was rare that the traffic on any of the lanes moved any faster than 8mph.

He watched the news. Guinevere was everywhere.

According to the news, she had travelled in the carriage next to him and yet he hadn't noticed her at all. Neither had the wrist pad alerted him to her proximity.

She should have been in Sydney.

The version of her presented in the news was an idealised one, to say the least. In reality she had been a broken reed, a robot with mangled and unfixable circuits. None of the obituaries mentioned her campaigning for the legalisation of HX-212, the awareness-enhancing drug. In the news, she was the poster girl for the Order of the Youth, her travels, charity work in the Outworld, all good things she had done—some of which he had never heard mentioned—brought to the fore. In her death, the prodigal daughter of the Order had become one of its patron saints.

Edward's mansion was situated in a quiet, leafy patch of an expensive street in Hampstead whose exclusivity was preserved by efficient-looking robot guards that screened him carefully before letting him through. Not even a loaded Neptunian bank account could automatically secure a slot here. To get one you needed high-level connections—Edward's mansion was sandwiched between the palaces of two former Prime Ministers.

Isabel opened the door. Her eyes were red and swollen. Nathan put his arms around her and held her. Isabel wasn't known for expressing affection through hugs, but this time, she didn't resist.

McKinleys had always been heavily involved in the British politics, religion and military. Their longevity was derived from histories that extended far back into the mists of time.

Isabel came from another druid family, slightly less prominent than McKinleys but with no less pedigree. In her youth, she had been the 'it girl' who had epitomised the post-Do-Muzude chic. She had lied about her age to get a modelling job that had involved simulated sex with pleasure robots. Her first ad was still used in universities as a case study of a flawless advertising campaign.

She led him to the reception room where Nathan sat down on a red gentleman's wing chair, not the most comfortable of seats for your bum but that wasn't something to expect from a piece of furniture that had been manufactured over four hundred years ago. Isabel's hand shook as she lifted her teacup.

"What was she doing in London?" Nathan asked. "I thought she had already left to Sydney."

"Yes, she had. According to the police, she flew back in the morning of the train crash. I don't know why. Anyway, that doesn't really matter. She's gone." She put her teacup on the table.

"There will be a state funeral at Westminster Circle this Saturday. Before that, there will be a wake here, starting on Friday evening at 6pm. Also, we will have a family meeting tomorrow, to discuss the arrangements. I hope you can make it."

"I'll be there. I'll be going to Oxford tonight but I'll be back for tomorrow."

He hadn't finished the tea yet when he saw a black government limo hoverer descend and stop in front of the mansion. The robot chauffeur came out and opened the door for Edward.

"Nathan! What a delight!" he said when he entered the reception room, but if there was any delight it was completely lacking from his voice. Aged sixty-three, height six feet two inches, a muscular body inside a sharp navy suit, Edward still looked every inch a soldier he once used to be. He had spent eleven years at the Royal Space Force, and his heroics for salvaging fifty-six hostages from the mines in Mars were part of the space force's modern mythology.

Less known was that he had also masterminded the crushing of the Bosnian rebellion. The human rights court in Haag was still debating whether he should be prosecuted for war crimes; the trouble was that there wasn't much evidence left behind and most certainly, no living witnesses. Because of the lawyers he had in his disposal it was unlikely that the debate would end anytime soon.

"I'll have a short nap and then I'll be heading back," Edward said. "Don't expect to see me before midnight." He turned around and headed up the stairs to the first floor.

"Have you talked to her friends in Sydney?" Nathan asked.

"No. I don't even know where she was staying," Isabel said. "Maybe with someone called Sarah. I don't know her surname."

Sarah Goldwin had been one of her closest friends at the university. She had convinced her to leave the Order for Buddhism, the spiritual path she had tried to follow more or less faithlessly.

When Nathan got out he called Sarah straight away but got an automated message. He realised that it was still 3am in Sydney.

9.

The Old British Library was a short shuttle hop from Hampstead. A colossal red-brick building complex, it had been built well before the Do-Muzude. Its stockrooms had been constructed to withstand water, explosions and most plagues known to man, and they had resisted even the dirty, poisonous water that had covered London for two and half years. Copies of ninety-nine of every hundred books on the British Isles were stored within its vaults, most of which hadn't been visited by human beings in over fifty years. Unlike the New British Library, the old one was a real, physical place. It had been built hundreds of years before Al-el Aza, the first literary robot that had composed the first perfect novel, stage play, television show and screenplay after it had synthesised all the human cultural output that had circulated in the AllNet. Al-el Aza had wiped out whole cultural industries overnight but fortunately, created some new ones.

Some readers still preferred novels written by human authors, but not many. Human authors suffered from a perverse desire to write unhappy endings. Why bother with them when stories by robots always provided the optimum emotional ride, unexpected plot twists and happy resolutions?

Most of the books in the Old British Library had been written well before literature had reached its current zenith. There were over hundred million books there but none of them could be seen in the red-and-white brick entrance hall. The hall was as empty of humans as always; there was a robot receptionist and a few bored-looking guard robots paced around.

The majority of Londoners would have loved to replace the library with something like a Mega-Cube but the librarians still had some friends in City Hall, and those friends had been able, so far, to successfully lobby against any plans for the library's demolition.

Nathan took the lift up to the Manuscripts Reading Room. Neftalem, the old Eritrean librarian at the reception was reading a book when he got in.

"Is Sam here?"

Neftalem continued reading.

"Is Sam in?" he repeated, lifting his voice. Neftalem looked up.

"Hi Nathan! What brings you here?"

"Just passing by. Is Sam in?"

"He's in the basement."

He typed on the keyboard—the library still stuck with them—and refocused his attention on the book.

Its cover title read: *The Ancient Ethiopian Monasteries*. It looked brand new.

"I didn't know that they still print them," Nathan said.

"They don't. This copy is well over hundred years old. I'll be retiring in two months and going back to Ethiopia. Not much would have changed in a century, so the information should still be mostly good to go."

"When did you go there last time?"

"Never been after I came to London as a young boy forty-five years ago."

Sam walked toward them, and considering his fashion sense, he looked rather dapper. His stone khakis did clash with the lime neon shirt but for Sam this constituted a major effort.

"How's Susan?"

Susan and Sam had got married three years ago which had reversed Sam's descent into solipsism.

"She's five months pregnant."

"Congratulations! The cloning won't be necessary now. A girl or boy?"

"It's a girl. With hazel eyes and blonde hair, just like her Mum. But with an IQ of only 167."

"That's still in the top one per cent. And if she comes out as pretty as her mother, she will do alright in life."

"I hope. How was Nabta Playa?" Sam asked.

"Hotter than London. Freezing at night."

"Sounds like a holiday to me. Whilst you've been relaxing in the sun I have done some actual work."

Sam clicked his fingers and a sturdy archive robot that had shadowed him stopped on its wheels. It held a large book in its clutches.

"I have been doing some tidying up," Sam said, his voice glimmering with excitement. It seemed something special was about to be presented to him.

Sam wasn't any master of ceremonies, but there was some pomp in his movements.

The archive robot rolled in front of Nathan and handed the book to him.

The book was heavy, dusty and battered. Its covers had been made of animal skin.

"It is almost as good as the real thing. Even the dust is reconstruction dust."

Nathan touched the rough leather, caressing it with his fingers.

"It is an excellent reproduction," he admitted.

"It would be even better if I could have manufactured it during the week. The machines do jobs for the Order from Monday to Friday."

"Is it all in early Geez?" Nathan asked. He had noticed the faded letters on the cover.

"Yes. We have sent the original back to Ethiopia."

"How did you get the money for the reproduction machines?"

"From the Order. They wanted to use our expertise to work through some druidic texts. That's why they placed the machines here."

Good reproductions made the originals seem inauthentic.

"The original was part of the loot brought by the British army from Megiddo in Ethiopia around three hundred and fifty years ago. We have returned it because of the directive by the Solar Nations Cultural Heritage Board that compels any Solar Nation to return historical artefacts to their owners if their legal owner can be established. This one was sent back to meet the quota requirements. It went to a monastery near Mediggo."

"What is it about?"

"I have no idea. Our translation robots have been unable to decipher it. The absence of vowels in the early Geez has turned out to be an unsurpassable obstacle. What we know is that it was produced in the kingdom of Aksum, as you would expect."

"I thought they used papyri scrolls at the time." He resisted the temptation to open the book there and then. "I'll do my best with this. Listen, I need your contact in the Underworld to do something for me. A clean hack. It should leave no traces."

"I didn't hear that. But he will be in touch with you shortly."

Nathan had used the hacker's services once before. He called himself Snyder. Much of what was known about the Outworld remained outside the public domain, and it was a lot easier and faster to do a hack than gaining legal access to data about the Outworld even when the data needed no security clearance.

Nathan put the book in his rucksack, said goodbye to Sam and ignored the security robots that seemed agitated about him taking the property of the library away, but unable to do anything.

After leaving the library Nathan headed to the King's Circle hopper station.

His fingers were itching to open the book but he knew that without tapping into Oxford University's powerful language programs from home it would be impossible to understand the text—if Earth's best translation robots had failed, he would need help from some really powerful software.

There were only a handful of specialists in the solar system that would be able to get anything out of the book. First, there was Professor Matthew Godwark at the Center for the Ancient Mediterranean at the University of Columbia, one of the leading experts in early Geez. Then there was Dr Mary Hootstill at the Department of Ancient History of the Macquarie University in Australia, specialised in hieroglyphs but also capable of reading Geez and Sabean, the ancient language from which Geez had borrowed its letters. There was Dr Luke Harrison, on study leave from Oxford University and Professor John Parsnip from the University of Pennsylvania's Outworld Studies Center in Egypt. There was Mark Goodwill, a Harvard researcher, and Nathan himself, an Assistant Professor at Oxford University's Faculty of African Studies.

Up to now, not one of them had managed to get hold of more than tiny fragments of texts in the early Geez.

Inside the hopper, he ordered a cup of coffee, closed his eyes, ignored the gentle nudging from his wrist pad to think positive thoughts and let his mind drift to the Outworld.

There were many great memories but more nasty ones.

He had been to the Mount Garbage in Uganda, the five-mile high heap of leftovers from the Solar Nations, and witnessed the recurrent garbage slides that often killed thousands of people looking for anything that could be sold, and the toddlers that had lost their limbs in the acids leaking from the remains of household machines. These scenes were edited out from the news reports so that the people of the Solar Nations wouldn't feel bad about their consumerism.

He had fallen asleep long before the hopper made it to Oxford.

10.

Nathan let his back rest on the heavy oak chair. Edward and Isabel's dinner room had been taken over by the close family but what was missing was Edward.

Dad sat two chairs right from him and talked to Stephen, Guinevere's brother. He had barely said a word to Nathan who sat between Isabel's sister Alice and Andrew, another cousin. The seat opposite him belonged to Isabel's but it was vacant.

Stephen was still wearing a City suit.

Traditionally, most banking had taken place in an area called the Old Square Mile, and many bankers still travelled there today but the location had little to do with trading and more with status.

All trading nowadays took place in the AllNet.

Stephen was a senior investment banker at the Milky Way Bank and traded with solar futures and the most speculative of products, the alien derivatives.

Nathan eavesdropped into the conversation between Stephen and Dad.

"We have moved on," Stephen said. "The traditional model of rebirth doesn't really fit with what we know about the nature of consciousness. Don't you agree that time has come to shake some of the druidic traditions? Really, soul can be broken down into a binary code. If that's done, rebirth becomes simple downloading. Where does that leave concepts such as Avalon and

Hades? Or gods? Maybe gods are just a soul in a prehistoric cloud."

"Interestingly," Dad said, "the old druidic texts don't refer to the human body as the inevitable and the only habitation for man's soul."

Often it was hard to tell what Dad really believed in. His philosophical pondering sounded much more liberal than his more fundamentalist public statements. In Dad's view it was the job of the druids to wrestle with the finesses of diverse and often contradictory dogmas of the various druidic schools and let the souls of the believers rest in the assurance of the afterlife.

They had been at the table for around forty minutes before Edward finally turned up. The religious small talk ended and the conversation switched to Guinevere's funeral arrangements.

"She will be clothed in a traditional white linen robe," Dad said. "I think she should also wear the jewellery of a druid priestess, unless you think that's an overstatement." His voice betrayed no emotion.

It had taken Dad twenty years of apprenticeship, five years as a druid and another ten years in the advisory circle before he had been elected to be the chief druid.

Most of that time had been spent away from home.

That was enough to drain all emotions out of anyone, although Dad had the ability to display any emotional state at will, but only publicly.

The chief druid had lost much of his power over the centuries.

Five hundred years ago Britain would have gone to war for one word from the chief druid.

One hundred and fifty years ago the Parliament would still have considered his advice seriously.

Now the chief druid's main task was to be the guardian of the ship that took the souls of the dead people to the afterlife, a ship of whose existence a large chunk of the population was sceptical about.

But nothing galvanised the chief druid's position more effectively than national grief. The presence of death had the power to make people believe in the afterlife.

Regardless of the malaise of the public status of the Order, the forecasts about the disappearance or death of the Order were misconceived. True, the Order practised its influence over an ever-eroding community of the faithful. But it had never derived its real power from spirituality or from its seats in the House of Lords.

The Order's power came from land ownership.

It was a little-known and little-advertised fact that the Order was the largest landlord on the British Isles. It owned the freehold for thirty-five per cent of the British soil, much more than even the British government. Year after year, it was getting richer and richer, regardless of how many or few followers attended the temple services and placed money in the offering circle.

Nathan's mind started drifting away when Edward and Dad began discussing the intricacies of the funeral procession's entrance to Westminster Circle. This was until Stephen mentioned the last time he had met Guinevere. That took everyone by surprise and pushed the conversation to a completely new direction.

"I might know why she flew back. Around two weeks ago, I saw her at the Liverpool Street underground station. She was there with an Italian man. They seemed close."

"It could be a new boyfriend," Isabel said. "Had you seen him before?"

"No. And I was in a train that departed. It was only my wrist pad that alerted me to her being close."

"Could that be Luzio?" Edward asked.

"Who is Luzio?" Isabel asked.

"A while ago, she asked for some money to help a friend out. She said his name was Luzio."

"Do you know anything about him?" Stephen asked.

"Not much," Edward said. "But if he is in London he should have heard about her death."

"Has anyone tried to call or left a message?" Stephen asked.

"Not that I know." Isabel said, "In any case, that will not bring her back."

Edward ate fast and wiped his lips with a napkin.

"Michael is here now, and he is more capable than I am to deal with the funeral arrangements," he said. If there was any sarcasm in his voice it didn't show. He got up and put his suit jacket on.

"I need to be at the anti-terrorism meeting in half an hour."

A long, black government hoverer had just landed and was waiting for him outside.

"Edward, can I ask you for a favour?" Nathan asked. He had delayed the question but now it seemed like the last chance.

"Someone needs to do the Buddhist rites for her. After all, she was a Buddhist. I can do that."

Edward looked at Isabel. She nodded.

"You can do that at the wake. A lot more discreet than having the Buddhist monks around. That would be a lot more conspicuous. But keep a low profile," he added. "It's only because that's what she would have wanted." Then he left.

"You have fifteen minutes," Isabel said. "That's when everyone else will be having tea."

"The procession and the funeral will be broadcast live in the AllNet," Dad said, steering the conversation back to the funeral.

"The Order has an advertising package that will cover the production costs and make some profit. The production team meeting will be taking place tomorrow morning." He glanced around the table. "Does anyone want to come?"

The disinterest was obvious.

"In that case, please let me know tomorrow by noon if you have any additions to the program. Rescheduling later will be impossible. Also, the production team will need to get Edward's speech by the end of tomorrow. My speechwriter can draft the speech for him, in case he is too busy."

Nathan said goodbyes when others started to discuss the flower arrangements. He took a taxi to King's Circle, a city hopper from there to Oxford Central Station, and walked home from there.

He hadn't checked his messages all day but did that at home. There was a message from John Sweetnail, the Professor of Akkadic Languages in Harvard who wanted to meet up with him during his visit in Britain.

Lola had also sent her consolations. She had met Guinevere once.

There was a message from the chief druid's aide running through every minute detail of Guinevere's funeral at Westminster Circle. His wrist pad had recorded the message two hours before the meeting with the family had even begun.

There was nothing from Sarah Goldwin.

11.

Nathan sat at the kitchen table and sipped coffee. It was 9.25am. He had slept restlessly, woken up by a hazy nightmare, somehow linked to the Indian girl in the train, but he couldn't remember any details.

In front of him on the table was the book that Sam had given him, and he was determined to get started with it.

Nathan's interest in Geez had originally been triggered by Abebech, the Ethiopian lecturer who had taught it at the University of Oxford. Abebech had had the most beautifully manicured and shaped pair of eyelashes and at fifty-five she had still been capable of turning heads. She had taught him for three years, up to the point he had exhausted all she had learnt, and surpassed her.

By that time his affection for Abebech had already been transformed to deep love for a dead language and its beautifully drawn letters. He had read every manuscript in medieval Geez archived in the Old British Library, around eight hundred altogether, and every fragment of early Geez he could find in the world, becoming one of the world's foremost experts in the process.

Why bother?

He had stopped asking that question long ago.

His studies had taken him to Ethiopia and to other parts of the Outworld. After exhausting all the sources in Geez he had turned his attention to other African languages, studied Bedouin cultures, and finally ended up in Nabta Playa at the Nubian Desert where he had encountered the ancient stone circles.

Man had to be able to live with some unanswered questions.

He had figured out that he enjoyed wrestling with facts that didn't come to him in the usual orderly fashion, in some premeditated formation made easily digestible by the AllNet. He rather preferred facts nearing him seemingly haphazardly, in fragments and with gaps.

Pre-packaged stories didn't interest him. What made others nervous and anxious gave him peace.

Perhaps it was due to all the drugs he had taken in his youth.

Not much was known about the origins of Geez. Its writing system preceded the syllabic writing that had come to Ethiopia some 2,800 years ago. The early forms had no vowels but later on, single vowels had been incorporated into each phoneme.

The text in front of him was early enough to have no vowels at all.

The book's physical form looked authentic and yet he knew that its molecules would have taken their current configuration only few months ago.

It felt even more real than the real thing.

The texture of the paper felt rough. The copy had a faint smell of mud. The original had been buried in mud that had dried and encapsulated it, protecting it from decay.

It had been cleaned with a krypton fluoride laser emitting at 248nm, an old but reliable technology. The beam had been put through a mask with a rectangular slit to cut out the lower-energy portions, and then focused through a lens with a 200mm focal distance, creating a spot on the document of 1.3mm x 4mm. The average energy density delivered was 30 mJ/mm2, and the 170-mJ pulses, at a repetition rate of 9 Hz, lasted only around ten nanoseconds each. Approximately 94% of the ultraviolet radiation delivered to the document would have been absorbed by mud, exceeding the binding energy threshold of the contaminants and causing dirt to break into particles that were blasted away.

He knew every intricate detail of the process as he had once spent a summer as an artefact cleaner.

Mud had bitten its way through the cover and the edges of the book before the encapsulation process had protected it. Fortunately, most of the inside had remained fairly intact.

The delivery notes stated that the original book had been looted with thousands of other books by the British army from Mediggo. The books had included an Ethiopian account of the unsolved mystery of the vanishing of the Ark of the Covenant from the First Jewish Temple in Jerusalem. According to Ethiopian histories, Menyelek, the son of King Solomon and Queen Sheba had stolen the ark from the First Temple and taken it to Aksum in Ethiopia. Nathan didn't put much weight on the Ethiopian account, but it was true that the references to the ark had disappeared from the Jewish religious writings around that time.

Most historians believed that this was due to the Babylonians destroying the ark when they ransacked the temple but the evidence for that was as scanty as for the Ethiopian version. Whatever the story's origin, the Ethiopians seemed to believe it, and even today thousands of small replicas of the ark littered the countryside and towns of Ethiopia.

When it came to the language of the book, most linguists hypothesised that it had evolved from Sabean, an ancient language spoken in the southern Arabia.

The first line of writing was read from left to right, and the next one ran from right to left.

He had already run the text through Oxford's computers, which had narrowed down the possible interpretations to a manageable number.

"This is the story of the master, a son of god."

That was his first, rough interpretation of the first line, and although he found no reference point to it in the Ethiopian religion, the interpretation still rang true.

His wrist pad alerted him to an incoming call. It was Sarah Goldwin. She was an Aussie blonde with reddish skin and cute laughter wrinkles on her cheeks and under her eyes, burnt there by the sun.

"How's Guinevere?" she asked. "I was so disappointed when I found out that she's not coming."

"You don't know what has happened? You must have heard about the train that blew up in London. She was in that train."

"How is she?" she asked. Her astonishment appeared genuine.

"She is dead. The medical crew got her out too late. The condition of her brain had already deteriorated beyond resuscitation."

"Oh my gods!"

"I thought you knew. I have been trying to get hold of you to tell you about the funeral arrangements. The funeral will be this Saturday."

"Holy macaroni!"

"What did you mean when you said she didn't come to Sydney?"

"I got a message from her, a day before her scheduled arrival. She had to postpone the trip."

"Did she give you any reasons for the delay?"

"No. She said she would explain later."

Nathan sat opposite Victoria in the café on the fifth floor of Harvey Nichols, the historic department store in Knightsbridge. A robot waiter hovered around, picking up dirty dishes.

Victoria had soft blue eyes but right now they were full of unease. She was tall, slim and chic.

Nathan forked another piece of cheesecake into his mouth and listened to her; only she wasn't talking.

"It must have been last winter, in Hyde Park, when I saw you last time," he said, trying to kick-start the conversation. She didn't respond. "Listen, I am trying to patch together the last week of her life. I need to know if you know anything."

"I know she's dead. Is that not enough?"

"Isabel said that she flew back from Sydney in the morning of her death. Yet, she never went to see Sarah. Wasn't she supposed to stay with her? Do you know where she could have spent the last week of her life?"

Victoria played with the piece of cheesecake on her plate, pushing it around with her fork.

"She sent me a message after landing. She said she would be staying in a hotel."

"Did she tell why?"

"No. And I didn't get a chance to talk to her. It was only a recorded message."

It seemed that she might have made it to Australia after all.

"Was she going out with an Italian? Luzio perhaps?"

"I don't think so." She flashed a feeble smile. "She was fast with boyfriends. But not that fast. She had just broken up with Gavin."

"Who's Gavin?"

"Gavin Morrison, the architect. He specialises in planning habitable structures for extra-solar planets. He is also a total asshole. Traveling on-board 55 *Cancri* 1, I think, so Earth will soon be a nicer place. Cute eyes."

"There is something else you aren't telling me."

Victoria glanced at him, hesitantly.

"Yes. There is something else. With her bipolar condition she always had her mood swings, as you know. In the last few weeks they got worse. She was becoming increasingly paranoid. She was sure someone was following her. The main reason for her heading to Sydney was her concern for personal safety. What I don't know is what could have brought her back."

"Did she tell you why she thought she was being followed?"

"She said she knew too much, I just don't know about what. I wished I had been a bit more inquisitive."

"Thanks for telling me that."

"No trouble. You can always go to her apartment if you want to have a look. I can give you a guest key. Just be careful."

"Thanks. I'd like to look in."

Victoria lifted her wrist pad and pointed it at him, scanning his iris.

"My lunch break is over. I have to go now," she said. "I'll see you at the funeral."

He kissed her on the cheeks; she walked off without looking back. A robot waiter served him another cup of coffee.

Like Mum, Guinevere had gone missing a few days before Midsummer. Mum's naked and mutilated body had been found deep in a forest near Oxford a week later.

Guinevere had died in a train. What had disturbed him was that his wrist pad hadn't alerted him about her proximity in the train and Stephen's remark about spotting her due to his wrist pad had reminded him of that. Now it seemed possible that she hadn't even worn hers because of her paranoia.

The only problem with this theory was that Guinevere's wrist pad was an implant. It monitored her health, and it would have been very difficult to remove. Due to her illness it passed medical data to her doctor.

She would have been unable to remove it unnoticed without a help of a hacker.

The chances were that she was still wearing her wrist pad.

He finished the coffee, left for a train from Knightsbridge to South Kensington and when he got there he changed to a District line train to Wimbledon.

Guinevere's apartment was located only a few minutes' brisk walk from the Centre Court and the Temple of Tennis. It was on a top floor of a white detached Edwardian house and opposite to a vast, green park on a leafy side street.

You couldn't find a better spot to live in London.

The front door lock scanned his iris and the door slid open. He took the lift up and by the time he got up there was a household robot welcoming him at the door.

He wasn't quite sure why he had come. It wasn't as if he expected to find anything here that would support whatever conspiracy theory she had been obsessed with.

No. What had brought him here was an almost non-existing hope of finding any signs of her return to the house.

He didn't find any clues. The household robots tended to keep apartments so neat that it was impossible to keep them messy for anything longer than few hours.

He sat on the sofa to think.

"Are you Nathan McKinley?" someone asked. He turned around to see a three-foot tall household robot behind him.

"Yes."

"I have already confirmed your identity but it is only polite for me to introduce myself. My name is Edgar. Guinevere asked me to talk to you. Only you."

"What is your message?"

"To begin with, because of her death, my ownership has been legally transferred to you."

"Shouldn't we ask Edward and Isabel about that?"

"No. Guinevere was my legal owner and she has transferred my ownership to you."

That sounded like typical robotic communication. If their owner had asked them to do something they would insist on doing that, usually rather politely, but so stubbornly that eventually anyone's resistance would wear out.

What would he do with another household robot?

But then, it had been Guinevere's wish for it to be given to him.

He should respect that.

Besides, the robot would remind anyone and everyone of that until it got what it had been programmed to ask for.

It occurred to him that now when he owned the robot, he could put it to some use.

"Has anyone been here after she left to Sydney?" he asked. "Be truthful."

"Her family has not been here, but the police came in yesterday. They looked through the apartment and removed some items, including her central computer."

"When did you see her last time?"

"That was over two weeks ago."

"Did she pack for travel to Sydney?"

"She did pack." Edgar wheeled around nervously. "Why don't we start going to Oxford now? Isn't that where you live?" it asked. "I'll get you a taxi. We can talk on the way."

For a household robot, Edgar behaved obnoxiously but there was an undertone in its voice that made him oblige.

When they got out there was no taxi in sight.

"We need to take a little walk. I have ordered the taxi to pick us up from the station."

"Why all this hassle?"

"The apartment is bugged and I would be amazed if the people who were after her or the police couldn't listen to us in a taxi."

Amazing! Guinevere had managed to infect her robot with paranoia!

They walked along the street, Nathan and a three-foot tall yellow household robot, not that infrequent sight, although in this part of town the residents hardly ever went to shop for their groceries themselves. Shopping with your household robot was for poor middle classes.

"Guinevere left home but not to Sydney. I could track her until around fifty miles from London. To near Oxford. But then the location services of her wrist pad were jammed."

"How do you know that?"

"I might look like a silly household robot but I also monitored her health. I ensured that her medication reached the bloodstream at predetermined intervals."

"When did she die?"

"On Friday 17th June at 4:03am, four hours before she was scheduled to fly to Sydney, her pulse and breathing slowed abruptly. The reading through her wrist pad gave me an indication that she was in a sedated state from Friday 17th June 4:03am to Saturday 25th June 11:46pm. At 11:46pm she was abruptly woken up, and her body went through a sudden increase in blood pressure, pulse and sweating. At exactly 12:00am, after 14 minutes of increased bodily functions, her heart stopped."

That was a full week before the explosion in the train. If Edgar was right, there was no way she could have died in the explosion.

"Are you sure about that?"

"I am absolutely certain, as certain as a robot can be."

"Where did she die?"

"As I said I don't have the precise coordinates. But whoever jammed the location services was unable to block the health data stream. Or they were unaware of it. After all, using a household robot as a personal health monitor is unusual. Or they didn't care."

"Why didn't you alert anyone for help?"

"It would have been useless without knowing where she was."

So, according to Edgar she had never travelled to Sydney and she had died a full week before her body had, allegedly, Nathan had to admit, been found in the wreck of the carriage.

"Her unconscious state was caused by a sedative," Edgar added. "She was woken up by an anti-sedative, deliberately. Her last fourteen minutes were spent in extreme pain. She knew she would die. Yet, she was not trying to escape. The data indicates that she was unable to do so."

"How did her life end?"

"Her heart burst. It seems clear that her death came when her heart was penetrated by some sharp object, perhaps a knife."

Nathan felt like he was about to faint. He sat down on the bench that faced the adjoining park. He pulled the oxygen can out and breathed its contents in slowly.

"What should I do now?"

"You should take me home."

They walked to the station and got in the taxi that was waiting for them. It flew them to Oxford, an expensive ride but the fastest way to get home. At home, Edgar sniffed around the rooms on the ground floor, climbed up the stairs to the first and second floor, and looked slightly worried. Nathan knew that the robots had no emotions but right now it looked like it was in exile.

12.

The ten directions converging, each learning to do nothing. This is the hall of Buddha's training; mind's empty, all's finished."

For a split second, Nathan's mind could conform to the old Zen Buddhist wisdom, but then it started running rampant. He had worked hard to clear his mind, to no avail. The only effect of meditation had been to bring up things from the past, memories he had long suppressed, nasty shadows from a time long gone.

Dad closed the door in front of him. Nathan was left standing in the corridor.

Alone.

He tried to hear through the thick oak door but the voices were muzzled. He went to the kitchen, and watched a Tom and Clinton cartoon. It didn't comfort him much; he was still wondering what was taking place behind the closed door. When the policemen finally came out, they wore pity on their faces.

He knew that the visit was about Mum. He had figured out that much. She had been gone for over a week. He had learned later that the police never send robots to deliver bad news.

Only the living knew how to talk about the dead.

Through the week it had been Dad who had dressed him up, made the breakfast, helped him brush his teeth and taken him to school, rather than the robots. He didn't complain when Dad served the oats with cold rather than hot milk. He reckoned that whining could just keep Mum from coming back. In the afternoon, Dad left his work early to collect him from school and take him back home.

Every day, he would run through the hallway to the kitchen, hoping to see Mum there, praying that she would be there.

Dad stood in the hallway. "Mum won't be coming back," he said.

"Why?" He could feel his heart pumping like a frightened hamster chased by a cat.

"She has taken the final journey to the Otherworld. It is the happiest place in the whole universe."

He had heard stories about the Otherworld. It was Mum who had told most of them. Bad people went to Hades, good people to the Otherworld. Some people believed that both the good and the evil were reborn, she used to say; the trouble was that it was hard to recognise them.

He felt hot teardrops rolling down the cheeks, bringing the taste of salt onto his lips.

"Why did she leave?" he asked.

What do you do when you are the chief druid but you don't believe in the Otherworld? You keep on doing your job and don't tell anyone.

That was Dad. In the end, no one alive had ever seen the druidic pantheon of gods. It didn't make much difference whether the chief druid believed in gods or not, as long as he served the people well.

"She loves you a lot but she had to go," Dad said.

That was the precise moment when he had lost his faith but it had taken him ten more years to understand it.

"Why can't I go to the Otherworld to be with Mum?"

"One day you will. But for now, we need to take each day as they come. You will feel better soon."

Dad glanced at the message on the screen of his wrist pad. "I have to go. The babysitter will be here any minute. I have so much work to do," he mumbled.

Nathan climbed the stairs up to his room, switched the lights off, and cocooned himself inside a duvet. He stared at the reflection of the full moon on the wall. He watched the moon and wondered if he would ever be happy again. Even the moon seemed sad.

13.

This body is the Bodhi-tree. The soul is like a mirror bright. Take heed to keep it always clean. And let no dust collect on it."

The old Buddhist saying came to Nathan's mind as he stood inside Westminster Circle and watched the funeral procession float in.

Westminster Circle was the most magnificent stone circle in Britain, the flagship circle of the Order. Its exterior was made of sandstone, mimicking the stones of Stonehenge. The decorative thick stone pillars that, according to the archaeologists, had evolved from wood pillars, stood two hundred feet tall, making every other construction around except Big Ben seem like dwarfs.

Westminster Circle was a super-sized circle with walls and a roof and it had a reminiscence of a Greek temple rather than an open-air stone circle.

It had been erected by the madness of kings and the blood of slaves. For the last nine hundred years, the kings and queens had been crowned, married and buried there. The circle was the centre of Britain's official religion, and its location next to the Parliament illustrated how, once upon a time, religious decisions had been as important as the political ones.

Amazingly, the building had withstood the Do-Muzude largely unharmed, a sign from gods, said the devout, a result of the government's needlessly expensive anti-flooding defenses around the building, protested the critics.

Westminster Circle was also the seat of the chief druid.

Nathan knew the liturgy by heart.

Soon, the thirty-one white coffins would appear, containing thirty-one bodies.

The rest of the victims had been foreigners or non-believers. The coffins would form a circle.

A circle within a circle.

The officiating druid, Dad, would stand in the epicentre, completing the Celtic cross, the symbol of the Sun, the sign of life. Everything inside the circle was covered in white, even the beards of the choir druids.

It was one of those moments when Dad looked his best. Gone was the impatient, grumpy perfectionist who drove his aides to despair with his many demands. Here was the charismatic, charming and elegant chief druid, the embodiment of the goodness of the Order, the man gifted in channelling the spiritual energies of the galaxy through his soul into the lives of the dead and the alive.

He was the one man who had the power to override the law of karma, to split cause from effect.

Occasionally, people fainted when he walked in.

Over three billion citizens of the Solar Nations observed the funeral live through the AllNet. Two hundred thousand more watched the event with twelve minutes' delay in Mars. Regardless of its slowly eroding power, the Order still knew how to stage a good show.

Nathan looked at the line of dignitaries, including Arnold Hargennegger, the prime minister, a tall, lean man with short brown hair. He had never seen him smile.

According to the early traditions of the Order, the Otherworld was located in some distant lands, or islands. That had sounded somewhat plausible until Christopher Columbus had sailed to

Americas, and soon after, there hadn't been any more islands to be discovered.

After another hundred years of expeditions, the exact location of the Otherworld had moved to the Moon, then to Mars, and now it was, allegedly, situated in another galaxy, although some thinkers reckoned it in fact lay constringed within one of the universe's many unexplored dimensions. Since Columbus every expedition had had at least one or two hopeful, fundamentalist druids looking for the Otherworld although they had no clear plan for what to do if they happened to find it.

For the vast masses of the people on the British Isles, the Otherworld was an old myth—in their minds, gaining eternal life through technology had become a lot more attainable goal.

According to the Order, the Otherworld had three regions: the land of the eternally lost, the land of health and youth, and the best, the eternal circle. You didn't want to end up in the land of the lost. It was the place where a soul, unable to be reborn, was attached to a body that had rotting limbs. It was a place where you were unable to live but incapable of dying.

Nathan washed his hands in the urn filled with cold water before he joined the circle.

"We meet today in sadness and joy to say farewell to thirty-one people who died two weeks ago," the chief druid said. "We ask for protection from gods, so that, as they begin their voyage to the Otherworld, their ship would not suffer wreck or storm. May their voyage be peaceful and calm! Fortunate are those who reach the shores of the eternal circle!"

The circle of mourners responded: "Do not weep for me for I have not gone. I am the wind that shakes the mighty oak. I am the gentle rain that falls upon your face. I am the spring flower that pushes through the dark earth. I am the chuckling laughter of the mountain stream. Do not weep for me for I have not gone."

Nathan recited the line without even thinking about it.

He had seen Guinevere two days before travelling to the Nubian Desert, the part of Sahara where Nabta Playa was located. They had met in a small Japanese restaurant near Bayswater in London. She had just broken up with a boyfriend, a Chinese stockbroker.

"Our greatest glory isn't in never falling but in getting up every time we do," she had said, reciting Confucius.

The man standing next to him in the circle tapped his shoulder. The prayers were over, the circle was moving, forming into a funeral procession that would end its journey somewhere in the sacred woodlands of Windsor. He wasn't planning to follow the procession. He wasn't a follower of the Order and as far as he was concerned, her soul had left her body long time ago.

Wherever her soul was, it wasn't here.

No, he had some business to attend, especially after what he had seen the previous night. He had to meet with Snyder as soon as possible.

14.

Guinevere's body lay in a coffin at the centre of her old room. The room was still decorated with the pink flowery wallpaper from her childhood, and there were still teddy bears on top of the antique drawer.

The lid of the coffin was open. Guinevere's face was bare but the rest of her body was shrouded in a satiny white robe. Her face looked like an angel's face.

Her neck was concealed under a broad brass necklace that had a line of Celtic trees of life engraved into it.

There were around fifteen people there, close family, friends and druids. Isabel stepped next to him. She was dressed in white from head to toe.

"The rest of us will go to have some tea and cake downstairs," she whispered. "The room will be empty for about fifteen minutes. It would be the perfect time to go through your rites." Nathan knew that Buddhist rites would offend any traditionalist druids in the room and there were quite a few of them there, in their white robes and beards.

"There is some tea and cake served downstairs," Isabel said loudly. "Also, Nathan wants to say goodbyes alone," she nearly whispered. "They were close."

Everyone else headed downstairs, except Edward. Nathan began by reciting a prayer from *The Great Liberation upon Hearing in the Intermediate State*, also known as *The Tibetan Book of the Dead.*

Tibetan Buddhists whispered the prayer to a dead body to smoothen the rebirth. He bowed over Guinevere so that his lips nearly touched her ear.

"Be not fond of the dull, smoke-coloured light from hell. This is the path, which openeth out to receive thee because of the power of accumulated evil karma from violent anger. If thou be attracted by it, thou wilt fall into the hell-worlds; and, falling therein, thou wilt have to endure unbearable misery, whence there is not certain time of getting out. That being an interruption to obstruct thee on the path of liberation; look not at it, and avoid anger. Be not attracted to it; be not weak. Believe in the dazzling white light."

He heard the door close behind. Edward had been standing there for about five minutes, probably spending every second in regretting his decision to let him go through the rites.

Edward still believed in the druidic gods.

Nathan stopped the recital and walked to the door. He opened it slowly and peeked out. There was no one in the corridor. He locked the door.

He went back to the coffin and lifted Guinevere's shoulders to roll away the linen cloth that was wrapped around her body. She felt cold and stiff, and the illusion that she was only asleep evaporated. He rolled the cloth up to her chest.

He had seen her adult body naked frequently, as Guinevere had been far from shy when she had been high, and she had been high quite often. It had been a beautiful body even after all that she had done to destroy it.

It didn't look so pretty now.

Someone had inflicted deep wounds onto her chest. There were at least a dozen of them. The sharp object had completely mutilated her breasts.

The stab wounds formed a nearly perfect circle.

He looked over her body for any other signs of violence and found many.

Her arms had been pierced with a sharp object, and cords, probably made of leather, had been pulled through her arms.

Edgar had been right about the pain she had suffered before her death.

He felt like vomiting but he had to check her body for one more detail. He unlocked the bronze necklace around her neck and removed it.

Over thousands of years, religious objects like that had been used to conceal a multitude of sins.

Guinevere's head had been severed from the rest of her body. The cut was neat, too tidy to have been caused accidentally.

He scanned her body with his wrist band.

He put the necklace back around her neck and rolled the linen cloth over her body like it had been.

He took a teddy bear, the one she had loved most, and placed it inside the coffin, next to her head.

He went to open the door, sat on the sofa, and waited until the other mourners came back.

15.

Nathan sat on the tatami on the floor of his Oxford townhouse, a house given by Dad for his twentieth birthday, just before Nathan had broken ties with him. The tightly woven rush grass mat, a Japanese import, felt cool under his bare legs. At nights when he was unable to sleep on the bed he came to the meditation room, and let its peace soothe the nerves. A solitary brass incense burner placed on the tatami spread the scent of sandalwood and cinnamon. One single touch of a button, and he could transform the interiors into whatever he wanted.

He preferred simplicity.

It was early morning and his mind travelled back to where his interest in meditation had started. Around ten years ago he had left the Himeji Castle, one of the few surviving Japanese feudal castles.

He remembered looking back, the morning sun lighting up the whitewashed walls of the castle that concealed a confusing maze designed to slow down the enemy's advance to the main keep.

The gates, baileys and outer walls were organised to force the attackers to travel in a spiral pattern around the castle, leading to many dead ends, and making them easy targets for the defending army.

The main tower, a seven-storied structure with tiered roofs still stood proud, withstanding the attack of time.

Like many tourists before him, he had been lost in the maze and asked for direction from an old Buddhist monk.

"Can you please help me to find the way out?"

The monk looked at him for a while, said nothing. He wished that his shaking due to the withdrawal symptoms from CX-12 wouldn't have been that visible.

"If you want to find the way out you must go to the Engyoji Temple."

He realised that the monk wasn't wearing a wrist pad and thereby had no translation aid.

"No. I am trying to find my way out of the maze," he said, now slowly.

"I know. Learning karate might have brought you here but you're still lost. You must go to the Engyoji Temple to find your way."

The monk's words sounded absurd but no more absurd than his experiences during his last CX-12 trip. Once he had found his way out of the maze he read about the temple and figured out that visiting it might be worth the trip; after all, he had come to Japan to see strange places, and the temple looked like it fitted the bill.

In total, there were 89,231 temples in Japan and the Engyoji Temple was one of the most difficult to reach. The climb up the mountain took about half an hour through a ropeway and by the time he reached the temple's forecourt by sunset he felt exhausted.

No other tourists had found their way there. He was the only guest. The monks asked him no questions but directed him to the eating area where they served him a bowl of noodles. After that, he was taken to the dormitory where he fell asleep quickly.

A coincidental event had taken him to the temple but it was its peace that kept him there, for months.

He had run out of CX-12. His mind didn't care but his body did.

It took him a week to work through the withdrawal symptoms, the last one a hammering headache.

He had been on a CX-12 trip at least once every day for the last three years, and waking up without a craving for another shot felt like being born again. Up to the point of getting through the last withdrawal symptoms the monks had largely left him to his own devices, only serving him noodles at meal times. Now, they began to pay attention to him.

He learned that the temple was over thousand years old. According to a local tale, Shoku, a Buddhist priest had seen a celestial being land on a cherry tree on the mountain. Inspired, he had carved a statue for Kannon, the Bodhisattva of Compassion, out of that tree. Then, he had built the temple. Since then the monks had been contemplating on Buddha's compassion there. Centuries later the temple had become the spiritual home of the Tendai sect, a branch of Buddhism that reconciled Buddhist doctrine with Shinto and traditional Japanese aesthetics. The Tendai sect believed in achieving enlightenment within one bodily existence, contrary to the other Buddhist schools. It also believed that that the phenomenal world was not distinct from Dharma, one's righteous path, and saw poetry and the arts, which many other Buddhists perceived as sins, to be alternative ways to enlightenment.

It was at the temple where he learned to meditate and it was to its memory where his mind wandered to when he needed inspiration.

He had sat inside the main temple building and stared at the gigantic statue of Buddha.

"Anyone who withdraws into meditation on compassion can see Brahma with his own eyes, talk to him face to face and consult with him."

He had meditated on Buddha's words but after two weeks he was none the wiser. He tried to improve his technique.

"Seat yourself on a thick cushion, putting it right under your haunch. Keep your body so erect that the tip of the nose and the navel are in one perpendicular line, and both ears and shoulders are in the same plane. Then place the right foot upon the left thigh, the left foot on the right thigh, so that the legs come across each other. Next put your right hand with the palm upward on the left foot, and your left hand on the right palm with the tops of both the thumbs touching each other."

A fly buzzed around, distracting his mind.

"If you feel your mind distracted, look at the tip of your nose; never lose sight of it, or look at your own palm; and let not your mind go out of it, or gaze at one spot before you."

At any other time he wouldn't have even noticed the fly; now it loomed large in front of his eyes, like the Earth's largest object.

A young monk passed him by and laughed. "You need to take this off," he said and pointed at the wrist pad. "With that on you can't get anywhere."

Nathan ignored his advice—for two days—and then he obliged.

The next few days were the worst of his life, a lot worse than getting weaned off CX-12. His mind became a strange place, an alien terrain with no familiar landmarks, nothing to hold onto. His thoughts lacked the luminosity that they used to have. They became dull and lethargic. Then he fell into despair. Determined, he ploughed on, and about a week later he noticed a tiny but discernible shift. His thoughts had become invigorated and they took new unexpected paths. The memories he had long suppressed came after him, chasing him along the dark alleyways of his fragile mind.

The skeleton of a tiny Algerian child on the dusty streets of Algiers after the Solar Nations had refused food aid because of Algerian terrorism; the teary eyes of the small girl that had lost her parents in a shootout between the Solar Nations troops and the Algerians at the Ahaggar Mountains. Walking through all that carnage and poverty, high on CX-12, with more money in the pocket than half of the surrounding nation and yet refusing to help anyone; he remembered doing that. He began to understand that whatever compassion was, he lacked it.

"Why are you crying?" an old monk asked when he found him there, weeping in front of the statue of Buddha.

"I am crying because my heart is as cold as stone."

"Don't cry! Be happy!" the old monk had said. "You have taken your first step towards understanding what compassion is. Come with me."

He followed the old monk to the garden. A monk, the oldest at the temple, was there pulling up invisible weeds.

"Have you ever talked with old Tetsui?"

"Yes. Why is he always so happy?"

"Do you know where the word 'Do-Muzude' comes from?"

"It means 'doomsday' in Japanese."

"Before the Do-Muzude, there was a Japanese doomsday cult that believed humankind was about to be decimated. Out of its ashes would come a remnant ready to reach a higher level of consciousness. The cult set out to speed up the coming of that end that would bring their salvation."

"I once watched a documentary about it. What's that to do with Tetsui?"

"He was their leader."

The old monk pointed toward a faraway mountain, barely visible from where they stood.

"The cult gathered there for their final battle. They broke into a government laboratory to acquire biological weapons developed secretly by the government. Tetsui had an antidote. The cult released the virus against the approaching Japanese army, and the resulting epidemics wiped out over one million civilians.

The army closed the area, and burned the land around the mountain, everything within a fifteen mile radius, to contain the virus.

Thousands of civilians vanished in the firestorm but that was considered to be necessary to stop the virus. Over one hundred and fifty monks who had been serving the villages around the temple were burnt alive."

Nathan looked at the vast, green land between the mountains and for the first time, he understood what a terrible price Japan had paid for one of its natural parks.

"The clean-up must have been super-fast."

"We do things effectively here. But many Japanese believe that this area is still cursed. In the end, Tetsui didn't have the courage to encounter death. He took the antidote. He escaped here to avoid the furnace. We let him in."

"And you are happy for him to stay here?"

"Yes. We are all trying to understand compassion."

His memories were so vivid that he had almost forgotten that he was in Oxford rather than in Japan.

He finished his meditation and walked down the stairs to the ground floor where Edgar was vacuum-cleaning the front room. When Edgar saw him it stopped.

"Listen carefully," it said.

"I can interfere with the listening devices in this house for two minutes; anything longer and it would cause an alarm."

"What listening devices?"

"Everything is connected to the AllNet. It isn't a one-way street."

It projected a recording of Guinevere on the wall.

She stood in her room and wore her customary cheerful dress; only her expression wasn't cheerful.

She looked deeply worried and anxious, nearly horrified.

"I am being followed," she said. "It all started with me digging into some deaths in the family. I am heading to Australia now. If you see this message it means that things have gone terribly wrong. You need to talk to Morris Chapman. He led the investigation of your mother's murder."

Guinevere's voice broke. "Nathan, be very careful. Nothing is what it seems."

The recording ended as abruptly as it had begun. Nathan was left staring at the empty wall.

"Your breakfast is ready," Edgar said, matter-of-factly. "Would you like to have some strawberry jam with your toast?"

16.

He sat in one of the dark, murky Underworld caves somewhere deep under Chinatown. The hacker whose name was Snyder had a long green hair and his skin tone was nearly white. He hadn't been above the ground for years. He handed Nathan a small box.

"You shouldn't wear them for more than eight hours in one go. Anything longer and you will be in danger of losing your sight. You can use them up to hundred times. They will fool any Customs scanner in the Outworld."

"One more thing. I need to break into the London Transport's central system."

"That is risky."

"Can you do it?"

"I said it is risky, not impossible. What are you looking for?"

"I want to know the passenger list of the train that blew up."

"Anyone specific?"

"Guinevere McKinley."

"That'll take at least half an hour. Get me a Venusiano from Café Galactica. With ice. That's the one thing I miss down here."

This part of the Underworld wasn't as filthy and disgusting as some others. It was a meeting area frequented by people from the overground—people who needed the services of the Underworld but weren't ready to plunge in deep into its alternative lifestyles. The Underworld sold plenty of services to the rest of the world, and the government let it run as a tax-free zone, content on taxing it indirectly through the customers.

Nathan walked up the sterile-looking corridor lit by green neon bulbs, took a lift then walked along another dark corridor until he got to a back alley in Chinatown.

There were no gatekeepers—the Underworld had no government but it existed in some sort of semi-organised anarchy where what mattered was respect. If you upset enough people through breaking the unwritten rules of the Underworld—no one seemed to be able to articulate the rules precisely—some sort of consensus emerged to sort you out.

Rarely that sorting out took a violent form but sometimes it did.

It was a world of conscientious objectors to regular society, shady criminals, folks that couldn't afford the steep London rents, homeless and illegal immigrants.

And folks intent on mutating beyond the limitations of human form.

It had been his adolescent experimentation with CX-12 and his work in the Outworld that had gotten him slightly more connected with the Underworld than most law-abiding citizens wanted to be.

The nearest Café Galactica was only about hundred yards from the exit but by the time he got there he was already sweating. He bought two of the largest-size Venusianos with ice he could find and walked back to the Underworld's entrance.

He walked along the dark corridor, took a lift and walked through another one lit with blue neon lights and to the little office or what else could you call that tiny space that no one seemed to own but could be rented for brief encounters. There was a double bed that indicated not all the dealings there were that detached but that some bodily fluids might change ownership from time to time.

Snyder was leaning over a small screen and seemed oblivious

to his arrival. Nathan looked over his shoulder and saw that he was working on a video recording taken in the train carriage. He put the coffees on the table but Snyder seemed to hardly notice them.

"There's something odd going on here," Snyder said. "Just watch!" He wasn't pressing any buttons and Nathan guessed that the screen was tapping directly into his neurons.

A fireball spread from the middle of the carriage into the rest of it and then the screen went black. Snyder rewound the tape. "Watch the man there, in the navy overalls."

The front of the young man's overalls had a logo printed on that said, "London Electric Fitters".

Snyder played the recording again, now in slow motion and he saw how the man blew up.

"According to the log his name is Robert Kelvin. He's thirty-five."

"So he was a suicide bomber?"

"Not quite."

"What do you mean?"

"He didn't commit suicide. I dragged out a lot more information about him, as I was intrigued about the explosion pattern. I hacked into the London Electric Fitters' system, and dug deep. According to them he had been working for them for seven years but it seems his identity had in fact been inserted only two days before the blow-up."

"So someone hacked into the system to get a bomb in."

"That seems pretty close to the truth. Only he didn't smuggle the bomb in. He was the bomb."

"So he had a bomb implant?"

"Based on the footprint of the explosion it is pretty clear that 'he' was 'it'. I am pretty sure that Robert Kelvin was an android."

"I thought that building them was illegal."

"Banning doesn't make the technology extinct. Only most people don't have access to resources to build them.

We are talking about a government or perhaps a major solar conglomerate here. "

"Who would want to blow up a train in London?"

"The list is long. There is a lot of money to be made from war and terrorism."

Before the Do-Muzude the American and Chinese governments had spent trillions in their effort to manufacture a robot that would behave and look like a human, but replicating the complicated facial expressions dependent on hundreds of tiny facial muscles had turned out to be a pie in the sky.

The Do-Muzude had put a stop to these efforts as all the resources had been geared towards clearing and rebuilding Earth and populating the habitable planets of the solar system. Mostly, the human-likeness of robots brought no competitive advantage to any business, and it was far more economical to produce robots that focused on specific tasks.

Also, most people preferred to know when a robot was a robot.

"What about Guinevere?" Nathan asked.

"I don't know how she died and where she died but one thing is certain. She didn't die in the train. She was never there. That's a mystery I can't help you with."

Nathan had guessed that much after seeing her body but there was a difference between probability and certainty.

Suddenly, the claustrophobia of the confined underground space hit him, and he found it difficult to breathe.

He pulled the oxygen can out of his pocket and inhaled deep.

He paid for the jobs and left.

Snyder had arranged the payment to go through a complicated series of multiple accounts opened in the Home Planets which should have made the payment nearly untraceable.

But nothing was untraceable in this universe. Snyder had just proved that himself.

He took the air shuttle back to Oxford from King's Circle and plunged straight into his research work.

If Snyder was right, there wasn't much he could do about the death of Guinevere right now.

Not before he had thought things through carefully and formulated a plan.

17.

Nathan woke up at 6am, ate light breakfast—fruit and porridge—meditated for fifteen minutes on the tatami, worked on new kung fu moves until he broke a sweat, went for a run, had a shower, watched the news. He worked on the translation until lunchtime, had light lunch, and then worked until the evening.

In the beginning of the translation work he had been able to establish the meaning of less than five per cent of the words in the text. By referring to books written in medieval Geez and the fragments of the Sabean language that had been found he had now managed to translate more than forty-five per cent. Gradually, more and more sentences and paragraphs had begun to make sense, and for the first time it seemed possible to transform mere conjectures into firm conclusions.

At the time when the British and the French had been called barbarians by the Romans, Aksum had been one of the world's four great empires, rivalling the power of Rome, China and Persia. Unfortunately, unlike with the other three, there was very little left of Aksum's glorious past. The British Museum where the treasures of other nations had traditionally ended up had only a few coins, pots and beads. The past of the once-great-nation remained one of the unsolved mysteries of the planet.

The most striking conclusion Nathan had gleaned from the

text was that it had nothing to do with the history of Aksum at all, although it used the language of the empire. It consisted of four stories about one spiritual teacher.

In essence, they were the same story but told from four different perspectives. The setting and the customs in the stories seemed more Middle Eastern than African.

There was some irony in the text being a story about yet another spiritual guru, although that wasn't unusual, as being connected to rites and traditions, religious texts had a lot higher survival rate than any other literary genre.

"If you have compassion on people you love, that has no value. Anyone can do that. If you give to people who give to you, that has no value either. Give to those that hate you, hoping to get nothing in return. Care for your enemies and you will be sons of god."

Parts of the text seemed to echo Buddhist teachings but other parts were distinctly this-worldly.

It was 10.25pm and already dark. He felt pretty satisfied with his interpretation but knew that at this stage it couldn't possibly withstand an onslaught from the academic critics. There was so much more work to do.

Suddenly, he felt empty inside. He had spent three weeks with the translation work and hardly left the confines of his apartment. He had even ignored messages from Lola.

The salsa music blasting from the loudspeakers flooded over Nathan's feeble attempt to resist Lola, who managed to pull him on the dance floor. The Cuban bar was as full as a Martian subway train during the morning rush, which suited Nathan well, as there was hardly any space to move around. It was the crowd moving him rather than his feet. Still, somehow Lola managed to dance beautifully. The air was hot and steamy, and as Lola pulled him closer his sweat merged to hers that smelled of cinnamon.

He took a wrong step, one of many, and stepped on her toes. She flashed a pained smile. He let his hands slide lower, fingers feeling the moves of her round hips under the red, tight dress.

Usually when he danced he felt like an apple snail that had strayed out of its shell, vulnerable and useless. Lola made him feel as if he wasn't that bad at all. It was an illusion that he wanted to last.

The bar was in the town centre, not far, and they walked home. Most people out in the streets were still on their way to the clubs. She leaned close to him, tried to keep warm, her dress far too minuscule to catch the evaporating heat from her body.

"Remember when I had a cocktail and somebody had spiked it with CX-12?" Lola asked. "You had to carry me back to the dormitory. My puke was all over your shirt."

"Those days, we would have been out until the wee hours."

"Thanks, Nathan. You always took care of me like brother."

Right now, Nathan didn't feel like a big brother, more like a big bad robot who wanted to devour the Red Riding Hood.

"Let's get a bottle of wine, something to eat, and watch a movie!"

They watched *Die Hard: Episode 221*. She had fallen asleep long before Wills the android cop had shot his way through the evil terrorists that had hijacked Mars, demanding ransom from the Solar Nations. He could smell her body as she lay on the sofa on her stomach, her buttocks two hills barely concealed by the red dress. Carefully, he removed her red heels, and covered her with a blanket. He knew she would be gone early in the morning, to catch the first city hopper of the day.

Nathan slowed the black hoverer down, turned off the motorway and began to follow the narrow country lane that was encapsulated by leafy hedges whose branches kept on hitting the windscreen. The fields around were being cleaned by robot harvesters; their steel casing glittered under the last rays of the sun. There was no space left to reverse if he were to encounter a tractor but at least the hoverer's booster would be able to lift it up to hundred feet for thirty-five seconds, long enough for the slowest and longest of the agricultural machines to pass.

He was looking for 15 Cottage Lane.

It had been easy to find out where Morris Chapman lived, another question altogether was whether he would be at home. There was no other way of finding out apart from visiting him, as he seemed to be completely disconnected from the AllNet.

A dead body swells. Exposed to the sun and wind, its skin turns blue before flesh begins to burst out. Then the body parts and intestines will begin to disintegrate. The body rots; its stink worsens. Worms find their meal.

That is what happens to the body according to *The Nine Visualisations of Uncleanliness*, a Buddhist meditation on a decomposing body.

That was what had happened to Mum.

He had been fourteen when he had discovered how she really died.

Three months after the funeral they had moved to London for Dad to be closer to his new job.

Dad had never sold the old house but Nathan had rarely been back there after the move. As far as he knew the old housekeeper still lived there.

He had been in Isabel and Edward's reception room.

"Poor Brid! She was in the wrong place in the wrong time." That was Mary, Isabel's friend, speaking.

Nathan detached his eyes from the chess board to see what she was referring to.

A news channel was reporting about a young woman whose corpse had been found mutilated in the woods, near Cambridge.

Her name was Alicia, not Brid.

Mum's name was Brid.

He focused on the chess game and pretended that he had heard nothing.

It took him three days to discover that all he had known about Mum's death had been one big, fat fabrication.

Oddly, he could find no references to the manner of her death in the AllNet, so he resorted to visiting the local library that archived old newspapers. The *Oxford Morning News* was still printed on paper. Hardly anyone read it but its publication was funded by the English Heritage, and it kept on running as the editor was dedicated to keeping the old craft of paper printing alive. He had hoped to find Mum's name in the obituaries.

He never made it to the obituaries. Her death had been front page news.

Her severely mutilated body had been discovered by a group of scouts in a forest near Oxford.

Dad came home after midnight. He came to check if Nathan was in bed.

"Have you done your homework?" Dad asked.

"I didn't go to school."

First Dad looked angry then worried.

"What?"

"I found out how Mum died. Why didn't you tell me?"

For a moment, Dad was quiet. "I am sorry," he said. I just wanted to save you from more grief."

He knew that Dad was right but that didn't make the deception justified.

Nathan turned to the farmyard, and parked the hoverer in front of a medieval thatched cottage. He got out, and stepped into the deep mud.

It always rained around here. It was odd how it never rained anywhere else but it always rained here. He didn't care about the rain but stepped over the mud on the tiny stairs that led to the front door. There was a mechanical doorbell and he rang it.

He waited for a while but there was no response. He walked around the cottage and peeked in from the kitchen window. No one was in but there was a slice of half-eaten toasted bread on the table. It didn't look like Morris Chapman had gone too far.

There was a flock of sheep grazing on a hill. There were also stables in some distance. The stables seemed a better bet for finding Morris than the flock of sheep with no shepherd.

An old green John Deere tractor stood in front of the stables, the kind that worked on diesel.

An old man with grey hair sat at the steering wheel. He wore green Wellington boots, brown cord pants, and blue quilted jacket. His boots were at the height of Nathan's nostrils, and smelled of horse shit.

"Nice tractor," Nathan started. "I saw one at the Museum of Technology. Where do you get the fuel from?"

"It comes through the English Heritage," the man said.

"I'm looking for Morris Chapman."

"Are you one of those goddamn reporters? You're wasting your time. That story is long-dead."

"I am not a reporter. I'm investigating the death of my mother."

"I thought Morris quit policing long time ago."

"The murder took place long time ago."

The old man looked at Nathan, and he could feel his piercing blue eyes trying to penetrate his soul. Finally, he stepped down from the driving seat.

"Are you here because of Brid McKinley?"

"How did you know that?"

"I can see the family resemblance. The last time I saw you, you were not much taller than a lamb."

"Are you Morris Chapman?"

"I haven't changed my name."

Morris started to walk toward the house.

"Let's go in. There's a storm coming."

Nathan had found out a little bit about Morris Chapman.

Fifteen years ago his career had ended with a corruption scandal, and he had retreated to the countryside.

"Why dig the past up now?" Morris said, as they came to the front door.

"My cousin Guinevere died at King's Circle."

"Sorry to hear that."

"She asked me to come to see you in case anything happened to her."

"I see." For a minute, Morris seemed to be in deep thought. "She did come here," he said, eventually. "I am afraid that her visit here might have triggered her killing."

"What do you mean?"

"It is a long story. I'll need a cup of tea to tell it."

Morris gestured Nathan to sit down on a sofa in the front room, and headed to the kitchen. Shortly, he came back with two cups of steaming hot tea.

"Your cousin was killed the same way as your mother."

"Is there some serial killer loose?"

"If things only were that simple."

"More than one killer?"

"It all goes back thousands of years. But there is a lot less enlightenment you'll find chasing this story than at the Engyoji Temple."

Nathan felt shivers run through the spine. His visit to the temple was hardly public knowledge.

"How do you know about that?"

"There isn't much real privacy when you wear a wrist pad. It all gets uploaded in the cloud. If you have means you can hack the cloud. And I still know some people in the police force."

He looked at Nathan. "I had to do that for my own protection. It wouldn't be the first time they send someone here. But we don't have much time. They know you are here. They can follow the signal from your wrist pad. Right now, I am scrambling it but that always raises suspicions."

"How did you know that I'd come to visit?"

"You looked for my address via the AllNet, didn't you?"

Morris handed him a bowl of chocolates.

"They are Martian imports."

Nathan picked a piece of chocolate and bit it. It had a flavour of hazelnuts and chestnuts, and a savoury undertone.

"That is how chocolate used to taste, before the GM cocoa seeds wiped out all the other crops. The original seeds for this chocolate were preserved under the ice cover of Greenland."

"Nice, nutty flavour."

"Have you ever heard talk about the Circle?"

When Nathan was sixteen, Dad had taken him to the Stonehenge Midsummer Festival, the last druidic festival he had ever attended. It had been made bearable by his second cousin's stash of CX-12 but otherwise it had been a forgettable affair.

He leaned on a monolith, and inhaled CX-12.

He noticed two druids in their white linen robes. He hid behind the stone, as there was a chance that they'd tell Dad about his use of drugs should they see him, and eavesdropped in their conversation.

"I'll be happy only when we get the last of them."

"There aren't that many left. One worked at the chief druid's office for the last eleven years. A member of the Circle at the heart of things! That caused a security alarm."

"What did they do?"

"They disconnected him from the cloud. He's in a mental institution."

"That was cruel." They burst into laughter.

"Never heard about it."

"That's not a surprise. Thousands of years ago, the druidic religion had two branches—the one that evolved into the Order, and the smaller branch, the Circle. The Circle was decimated soon after the beginning of the Roman rule. What sped it up was that the Order saw the members of the Circle as prime material for human sacrifice and collaborated with the empire to hunt them down."

"Why two branches?"

"The rift between the Order and the Circle has much to do with Brigid."

"The goddess Brigid?"

"Yes, the mother goddess of many European nations, the source of regeneration and abundance. The battle between these two factions began thousands of years ago because of the human sacrifices offered to her."

"So this is about wicker men?"

"Yes. And other forms of human sacrifice. It was the Circle that orchestrated the abolition of human sacrifices. It was at a time when the Order was split in an internal rivalry."

"So why isn't it attributed to them but the Order?"

"History is written by the victors and it was the Order that emerged victorious. It didn't take long for the different factions to reunite against the common enemy after the abolition. The known members of the Circle were hung, guillotined, crucified, and so on, for treason. The ones that escaped went underground."

"So what is the Circle?"

"The Circle is and has always been the pacifist, non-hierarchical strand of druidism. It has preferred to work things invisibly."

"I thought that human sacrifices were rare."

"And most scholars discount the stories about them as myths."

"Most myths are exaggerations of historical facts," said Nathan, slurping his tea. "Thousands of years ago human sacrifices did happen."

"Human sacrifices have been practiced in all continents and by many nations," Morris added. "The Aztecs and Mayas sacrificed human beings to attain good harvest. A Jewish king once sacrificed his daughter to gain victory in battle. Mongol and Scythian chiefs took most of their household with them to the Afterworld."

The sky outside was getting darker.

"The Etruscans held gladiator fights in funerals, as survival in the afterlife demanded a blood sacrifice. The Carthaginians sacrificed children to their gods. The Romans had various forms of human sacrifice before the Roman Empire exterminated these practices."

It was becoming clear how the worry wrinkles on Morris' face had been created. He seemed obsessed with killings.

"Vestal virgins were buried alive as offerings to the gods of the underworld," Morris continued. "The king of Edom offered his firstborn son and heir as a whole burnt offering. Norse warriors buried themselves with slave girls believing that they would become their wives in Valhalla."

"But gradually, these violent practices disappeared," Nathan interrupted.

"Not really, but we will get to that. But it wasn't just slaves that died. The Swedish King Domalde was sacrificed by his underlings to bring greater harvests and to win wars. His descendant King Aun killed nine of his sons to live longer. The Chinese gave young men and women to river deities and buried slaves alive. Once the Aztecs sacrificed more than eighty-four thousand prisoners in one day. The streams of blood covered an area of ten square miles. The dead victims were skinned and a priest would use the skins."

"Mankind has a grim history."

"It isn't just history. The Britons still pierce their victim with a blade and divine their future from the victim's death spasms."

"That practice was criminalised by the Parliament over thousand years ago," Nathan said.

"Yes and the next logical step was the abolition of slavery. But criminalising something has never stopped it. The human sacrifice was pushed underground."

"The official story is that the Order replaced sacrifices with prayers and financial offerings."

"And they are a lot more profitable to the Order. But you, what do you know about the stone circles? Isn't that something you're researching?"

"The ones in Britain or in Sahara?"

"The ones here."

"There are 702 remaining stone circles on the British Isles," Nathan said. "Who built them is shrouded in mystery. Some archaeologists think it was the first wave of the Celts that came to Britain but that is just a conjecture with no evidence. Around three hundred of them are still in use. The rest are derelict. Then there is Stonehenge that claims to be the oldest but isn't. The first circles were erected around five thousand years ago, and for the next 1,300 years, they popped up everywhere. What seems evident is that their builders saw them as gateway to the spirit world, to gods."

Morris pulled out a box of cigars. He picked one and lit it.

"Sorry for the smoke," he said.

Morris' cigar had a sweet, pleasant flavour that was slightly overpowering.

"The circles are spread evenly all across Britain but their shapes vary," Morris added. "They are nearly perfect circles in the south-west and north-eastern Scotland. Egg-shaped and elliptical rings with large well-spaced stones are popular in Cornwall, Devon, Wales and Scotland. Some had a stone in the centre, others didn't. And there are several superhenges with such a long diameter that whole towns have been built inside the circle."

"That's all interesting. But I came here because of my mother. And Guinevere."

"Your mother vanished a week before the Midsummer Festival, as did Guinevere."

Morris gestured Nathan to follow him. He walked to the

corridor and opened a door in the end of it. A weak smell of mould welcomed him. Wooden stairs led to a basement. Morris switched the light on and stepped down the stairs. Nathan followed him. The stairs led to a low room that had been turned into a library and study with its bookshelves bursting with dusty folders. Morris picked one from the desk. He handed it to Nathan.

"Open this only if you really want to know what happened to your mother. You *will* find the content disturbing." Morris stepped on the stairs.

"I'll go check the horses," he said. "I'll be back in half an hour."

Nathan glanced at the spine of the folder. It had a yellowing sticker with 'Brid McKinley' handwritten on it. He opened the folder.

When it came to filing it was obvious that Morris didn't like introductory pages. The first page was a transparent pocket with a picture from a crime scene. It was a picture of Mum's naked body that was partially concealed by forest undergrowth.

There were some close-ups.

The remains of a plaited leather band were still around her left upper arm. Both her arms had been pierced with some sharp instrument. Her chest had been mutilated, her nipples cut.

He knew these were pictures of Mum's body but they might have as easily been taken of Guinevere.

The accompanying police report informed that her body had been pulled out from a bog by a lone trekker who had wandered to the crime scene.

Nathan hardly noticed Morris' return until he spoke up.

"The man or woman buried in a bog will never reach the Otherworld," Morris said. "She would stay in an in-between state with the soul never departing."

"What would that achieve?"

"According to ancient beliefs, the bog is an in-between

world. Apart from criminals, some people were thrown in the bog as substitutes for their tribe's transgressions. The gravest of sins demanded the most precious of sacrifices. The soul of the punished or sacrificed would remain in a frozen state, never reaching the Otherworld. If you believed in this, you could only imagine the horrors that your loved ones faced, spending an eternity in a limbo state."

Morris glanced at Nathan with an expression that could have been deciphered as pity.

"Both your mother and cousin came from high-ranking druidic families. You can only imagine what type of transgressions their deaths covered."

"You are telling me that their deaths were ritual killings." Nathan felt anger and dread welling up within him. "And the people who did that are still out there."

"Yes. And I also suspect that your mother was killed at least partly because she was a member of the Circle."

"How can you know that?"

"I once belonged to it."

"You belonged to the Circle. What happened?"

"When you go out, look up to the sky. You'll see the drones circling the house. Or you would, if it were a sunny day. Right now they can't see much. Effectively, I've been isolated from the Circle by surveillance. Well, at least most of the time."

"If the Circle is such a secretive organisation how did you join them?"

"The Circle might seem invisible but it's never far from the Order. The members of the Circle believe that the Order was birthed from the Circle but lost its way. The Circle has no hierarchy. The Order has a top man, the chief druid. The Circle believes no man can stand at the centre of the circle. Only gods can. From the beginning, it detested the way the Order conducted sacrifices at the centre, in the space reserved to gods. But I didn't find the Circle. It found me."

"So, what happened to her?"

"I am not hundred per cent sure. Your family is one of the leading families of the Order, and they didn't get there by accident. In the Order, you get nothing free."

Morris took another cigar and lit it.

"You saw the files downstairs. My research goes back one hundred and fifty years. Each folder contains a suspected case of a ritual murder. There are hundreds of them."

"Why would they let you store this stuff, whoever they are?"

"It all goes down to over-reliance in technology. The spies are AllNet trained; they don't see paper as dangerous. If it doesn't have 24/7 access it doesn't exist to them, as it isn't accessible from all around the solar system. Besides, what do I really have? A dusty archive that can be burnt in a flash. As it is un-connectable to the AllNet it is un-distributable."

"So you have been collecting this information for decades."

"Yes and no. I scavenged much of this from the archives of the Police Central Information Bureau only hours before the archives were torched. The arsonist was never caught."

"Hasn't the Order stated that human or animal sacrifices have no effective value in the salvation of mankind? Is this some fringe group?"

"These people operate very rationally, and they are far from the fringe in the Order. They don't kill for pleasure. It is all strictly business with gods. The Order believes in the sanctity of human life. There is no purposeless sacrifice."

"If the sacrificed must represent her people it must be her tribe that killed her. Could she have volunteered?"

"I don't know. But the people involved would have been from her clan. In your mother's case, that doesn't necessarily mean McKinleys. She wasn't a McKinley. She was a Gillington. But the main point is that there is no individual killer out there. It is a whole clan, or at least some of the leading members. The culprits can be found in your family tree."

Morris got up.

"You should go now."

They walked up the stairs and along the corridor. A woman's portrait hung on the wall.

"That's Elvira, my wife. She died twenty years ago. Her hoverer was found in a bottom of a lake in Scotland. I didn't even know that she was in Scotland."

"How could Guinevere's body end up in the underground?"

"That doesn't fit the picture but not all the bodies are buried in a bog. Maybe someone wanted to give her a decent burial."

"How could these people have known about the explosion in advance?"

"Maybe they did, maybe they didn't. Maybe her body was never in the tunnel."

When he got out the storm was already rising. He let the autopilot take him through the narrow lane back to the main road. The raindrops were now huge, pounding the windscreen, and the wipers were struggling to clear the water.

The water washed away his assurance that Morris was right. The killings were real but that didn't necessarily mean that there was some sinister conspiracy behind them. He found it hard to believe that someone in his family could be involved in anything as gruesome as that. They were all political animals but that didn't make them into monsters.

18.

At home Nathan dived straight into studying the book. He didn't really want to work but the images of Mum's mutilated body haunted his retinas, and the only way to escape the ghosts seemed working to exhaustion.

He was now certain that all the four books were all translations from another language rather than written originally in Geez.

What he didn't know was whether they had all been translated from the same language or from different ones.

Perhaps there had once been one original text which had then been translated into many languages and later on translated into Geez with each translation multiplying the differences, so that the end result had been four different versions.

In all languages, some words appear more regularly than others, and those common words provide the firm foundation for expanding the area of certainty.

It was that foundation he had been building on.

His interpretation would soon be contested by other scholars and linguists. The humanist sciences were all about contests over the meaning of words, and the weapons of choice at these contests were words.

He had compared the texts with medieval forms of Geez that possessed vowels, and worked his way back to root words that didn't have them. It was pain-staking work that took an awful lot of time.

He had drawn from what little was known about the Sabean language that had lent Geez its alphabet. Drawing from a similar language had its risks as a word could be spelled in a similar way in both languages but have even an opposite meaning.

Initially, he had suspected that the original texts might have been Egyptian, as Egypt was clearly mentioned in the book. The main protagonist of the texts, the spiritual master, had been called 'a son of god', and that's what the pharaohs were believed to have been. Maybe that was what this was all about.

But the spiritual master looked nothing like a pharaoh. He did believe in the existence of the afterlife but wanted to make it accessible to all.

In Egypt, the afterlife had been the realm of the pharaohs.

The Egyptian religion centred on the pharaoh's preparation for the afterlife. The pyramids had been erected as star gates to send the son of god to heaven.

It had cost thousands of lives to build a pyramid in order to save one life.

Egyptian men had false penises attached to their mummies while Egyptian women had artificial nipples. In Egyptian understanding both would become fully functional in the afterlife.

The spiritual master had taught that women and men were equal in the afterlife. Maybe he had been an Egyptian religious revolutionary.

Perhaps that explained his violent death.

Or perhaps he had given Buddhism an Egyptian spin.

Like Buddha, the spiritual master had been a healer. Legends ascribed all kinds of miracles to Buddha. By washing his hands over the seed of a ripe mango he had caused a tree to spring up fifty hands high. Once he had flown into the sky with fire and water streaming from various parts of his body. He had performed these miracles to dispel the gods' doubts about his mission.

Had Sam not come across the book somewhere in the basement of the Old British Library, no one would have ever heard about the spiritual master's teachings.

Who was he?

He had said—if his translation was right: "You shall know if my teachings are true by putting them into practice."

This was reminiscent of Buddha who had said, "After examination, believe what you yourself have tested and found to be reasonable, and conform your conduct thereto."

Yet, in many ways these two teachers seemed miles apart.

Someone tapped his shoulder. He turned around to see Edgar. It put a coffee mug in front of him.

"Thank you, Edgar."

"You are welcome, sir."

"Did you like Guinevere?"

"Liking doesn't come to it. I have been programmed to like all people."

The coffee was perfect, as always.

He had had Edgar for only three weeks but he had already grown quite attached to it. Edgar never made mistakes with coffee.

Nathan lay on the sofa, soiling the white leather upholstery with his muddy trainers. Lawrence, the family psychiatrist with slowly receding hairline and round glasses scribbled something on the screen.

"Tell me what you feel, at that moment when you grab your rucksack. Do you feel a sense of dread, excitement, relief or emancipation? What are you running away from?"

Nathan rubbed the dirt from his soles deeper onto the white leather, which failed to change Lawrence's placid expression. With his fees he could buy a new sofa as easily as hair and eye treatment which he didn't, as he would rather look like Sigmund Freud.

"I'm not running away from anything."

"You were at the hopper station, buying a ticket to Oxford. That's heading quite far away from home for a seven-year-old boy."

"But that's where my home is!"

It was the robot station assistant that had spotted him to be far too young to travel alone that had stopped his journey, not the ticket sales machine that had gladly accepted the payment. Sometime after the assistant had taken him to custody, a human policeman had appeared and taken him home after a short and rather pleasant interrogation session.

They had taken him in a police hopper. At his request, the policeman had played the siren.

"Where is your home?"

"It is a large white house along Pinewood Lane, surrounded by apple trees. Round the corner from there is a sweetshop where Mum walks with me to buy Turkish Delights."

"You know that you don't live there anymore."

"Dad tells that when you die it is not the end. One day, you will be reborn. If Mum has already been reborn, she might still remember the way to Pinewood Lane. She won't know how to find the way to where we live now."

"There is nothing you can do to help her find you. If your paths do cross, you won't recognise her. Besides, she is still probably in Avalon."

Lawrence tapped his screen, and then glanced at the clock on the wall.

"Time is up," he said.

It was like he was following some strange code. Their meeting always took exactly an hour, not a minute less or more, no matter how much or little he had to say.

Dad opened the door without knocking. It was 1.00pm.

"Can I have a word with you?" he asked Lawrence.

Lawrence left Nathan to wait at the reception, while he spoke with Dad, behind the closed door. To kill time, Nathan played games on his wrist pad.

Dad took them back home in the hoverer. He was as quiet as usual, his mind probably wrestling with some work-related thing. Nathan licked the lollipop Lawrence's receptionist had given him.

"We need a holiday. Should we go to France, or Italy? Or, maybe we should head to Mars."

When the time for summer holidays had come Dad had taken him to the southern coast of Spain for a week. Most of the time, Dad had kept on working with his wrist pad, running the many operations of the Order. It hadn't been nearly as much fun as the holidays with Mum.

19.

For two weeks, the book had absorbed all Nathan's attention, and he had isolated himself from the outside world. Edgar had kept on tidying up after him and given him some company. To him, Edgar was becoming like a real person, a feat no other robot had ever achieved.

It was evening, and for the first time in few days he actually checked his messages.

The latest message was from Lola, recorded only two hours earlier. She asked him to call her straight away.

It was 11.03pm but Lola picked the call immediately.

"Hi Lola!"

"Have you seen the news?" she asked. "Or are you still so preoccupied with your research that you have no idea about what's happening outside your house?"

"I haven't watched the news."

"You should watch them."

"Which channel?"

"Any of them."

"What's it about?"

"Just watch."

Lola ended the call without any further explanation. Nathan went to the front room and switched on the large screen. He chose Galactic News.

A reporter stood in front of King's Circle underground station.

The commuters passed her without paying much attention to her. Next to her stood a young, skinny-looking woman with long, black hair.

"Two months ago a bomb ripped apart the underground train," the reporter said. "Needa was in the carriage that exploded. He survived thanks to an unidentified passenger who braved his way into the carriage and pulled her out. She was dead for five minutes but, fortunately, her resurrection was successful, mainly because she got the treatment in time."

She turned to Needa. "How has your recovery progressed?" she asked.

"I lost a leg and I had terrible internal injuries. The reconstruction process took two and half months. But he saved my life."

"Although we don't yet know the identity of the brave hero we have managed to find some footage of him."

It was then when it dawned on Nathan that he had met Neeta before. She looked very different now and Nathan could only guess whether she had been forced to get rid of her alien skin or if she still wore it.

It was a standard medical procedure to get rid of it if an injured Underworlder made it to the hospital.

The screen played footage of a young man ascending the escalator.

Although his face was partially covered with blood Nathan could still recognise himself.

"Please call us if you know this man!"

In the studio Alex Mithall, the police anti-terrorism specialist, sat on the couch. He looked uncomfortable.

The AllNet celebrity journalist John Whitehall, notorious for his barking and sniggering style, was about to interrogate him regarding the police's failure to catch the perpetrators of the terrorist act.

"It is nearly three months now and the police have yet to make any arrests. It seems that you don't even have any leads. How is that possible?"

"The individual or the group behind the bombing had some very sophisticated technology at their disposal. The inquiry does have some leads but at this stage we are open to all possibilities."

"Doesn't the use of sophisticated technology narrow down the suspects?"

"For operational reasons, I'm not able to comment on that."

Nathan hadn't spoken about what had happened, not even to Lola.

Nathan called Dad. When it came to dealing with the AllNet, the chief druid's media team would be the best possible ally.

If they were able to hide skeletons in a spaceship closet, surely they would be able to handle some positive news.

Fifteen minutes after he had finished the call an unmarked hopper from the Order landed on the doorstep. The robot pilot didn't talk much so Nathan spent the flight time admiring the views.

The hopper used a flight height reserved for the police and high-ranking government officials. It flew faster than any hopper he'd ever been in.

Dad had asked him to disconnect his wrist pad and not talk to anyone at all before he had been briefed by the chief druid's media team.

After ten minutes' flight time the hopper landed on the hopper pad of Lambeth Palace that was situated on the southern bank of the River Thames. Two druid guards escorted him to the palace.

For eight hundred years, Lambeth Palace had functioned as the residence of the chief druid and the spiritual if not always the operational headquarters of the Order. Behind the unassuming and rugged-looking medieval walls stood a vast complex of buildings and gardens. The buildings and its people oozed aristocratic self-confidence.

Hundreds of years ago, the river used to run wider and closer to the palace, and the only way in was on barge.

The word 'lambeth' came from the old English word "loamhithe", which stood for a 'muddy landing place'. There wasn't much of the mud left to be seen anymore.

He was escorted to the Blue Drawing Room where he waited. The room overlooked a garden filled with flowers in rainbow colours, gigantic ancient oak trees, ponds and a smaller, separate rose garden. The window was open and he could hear the singing of birds and smell the delicious scents from the hundreds of species of plants that had found refuge from the sweltering sun in the gardens moistened by Earth's most precious natural resource, clean water. Unlike the rest of London's gardens and parks that had been watered by filtered sea water for decades, the palace gardens were kept green by spring water from Scottish highlands flown in inside large tankers. The druidic traditions necessitated water from the sacred highlands—water that was like 'a precious sacrifice of the deep, sprinkled back on the earth to instigate rebirth', according to ancient druidic inscriptions.

Finally, Dad walked in with a handsome-looking man in a grey pinstripe suit. He had seen Duncan Loiter, an Australian-born spin doctor in countless of AllNet shows but he had never actually met him.

If you had to ask how much Duncan's services cost, you didn't have the money for them.

"Duncan will look after the media," Dad said.

"I'm looking forward to working with you," Duncan said.

"I'll leave you with Duncan," Dad said, and turned around. "He's a lot better in these things than I am."

Duncan sat down on the chair opposite him.

"We don't have time for an extensive makeover. The AllNet channels are already looking for exclusives."

How did they know to come to Duncan?

Duncan pulled a small steel box out of his breast pocket.

"You should take one of these pills around half an hour before an interview. "

"What are they?"

"Nothing you should worry about. There are no side effects. They sharpen your focus and make you relax. Perfect for interview situations."

"I don't need them."

Duncan put the box back in his pocket.

"As you wish. More importantly, your father doesn't want to put the spotlights on the fact that you have not been an active member of the Order for a while."

So the Order wanted to look good. No surprises there.

"The media circus will only last for a few days. After a while they will lose interest. You will have twenty-four hours to prepare for the first interview. Your father will handle the media until then."

"How long will it all take?"

"You will have your life back in two weeks. It would be best if you stayed in the palace until that."

"I'd rather stay with a friend."

The palace gave him the creeps.

"There are risks involved but we can handle them. Just don't speak to anyone before the first interview."

By the time Duncan's men had taken him to Lola's apartment in a rusty, nondescript hoverer all the media in the AllNet was aware of his identity, and people he'd never even heard about were taking their fifteen seconds of fame.

He watched with Lola how on one channel, a reporter interviewed someone who used to live on the same street in Oxford when he was a child. According to him, Nathan used to be one of his best friends.

In Galactic News it was Dad in the studio. He wore casual druid wear, designed by Duncan's subsidiary company.

No wonder he had been in such a rush.

"Nathan has always been like that," Dad said. "I'm not that surprised. He gets out of his way to help others."

"Why didn't he talk to the police?"

"It didn't look like a big thing to him."

The doorbell rang at 9.23pm, and the footage from the front door security camera appeared on the news screen.

"Do you know him?" Lola asked.

"No." Nathan had never seen the young ginger-haired man on the screen. He got up, went to the window and peeked out.

There were hordes of reporters, camera robots, lighting robots, and hoverers from all the major networks.

Galactic News, Solar Extravaganza, Hello, Old British News, Europe Today, Third Rock from the Sun; he could see their logos on the hoverers.

The floodlights began to climb up the wall. They had spotted him. Nathan closed the curtain.

"It might not have been such a smart idea for me to come here. I'll need to call Duncan."

20.

It was 8am, and the street was still empty of traffic. The night before, the reporters and TV crews had vanished fifteen minutes after he had called Duncan, and the neighbourhood had become eerily quiet. Nathan checked the local traffic news to discover that the whole street had been shut down due to a problem with a semiconductor line. Streets didn't get closed like that in London, not especially if there was no sign of any repair work, so he guessed that it had been Duncan's handiwork.

Nathan opened the window and peeked out. Both ends of the street had been blocked and they were guarded by robot cops that let traffic out but no one in.

Lola had left to work at 7.30am.

At 8.15am on the dot, a hoverer with dark windows parked in front of the house. He walked down the stairs and got out. A bulky-looking human bodyguard was waiting for him by the hoverer. He took Nathan's gym bag, put it in the trunk, and opened the door.

"Hello! My name is Kim! It is going to be an exciting show! The ratings will hit the roof!"

The annoyingly upbeat and unnaturally attractive Kim, one of the *David Moss Show's* Japanese hostesses, sat in the back.

Her dress, if there was enough material there to call it a dress looked like it was made of aluminium but yet it stretched like rubber.

Her lips were far too small and eyes too large for her perfectly elliptical face, and she looked more like a manga character than a real human being.

"Do you want a drink?"

"Some apple juice, please."

"You can get anything," she said, and opened the bar which seemed to hide a large selection of spirits and other drinks that, as far as he knew, were yet to be legalised.

The *David Moss Show* was the hottest ticket in town, a show packed with galactic celebrities as guests. Duncan had explained his AllNet strategy the night before.

"We'll take you to the biggest show in town. Maximum exposure with minimum work. The media will lose interest quickly after that. In two weeks no one will remember you, but they will have newfound affection for the Order because of your story."

Two weeks would be slow enough to create an image of an ideal family but fast enough to keep that image from cracking.

Right now it seemed like the only ticket in town.

Twenty-five minutes later the hoverer landed in front of Soho Studios where *The David Moss Show* was filmed.

When the hoverer door opened Nathan understood that Kim's costume served also as a distraction. The cameramen focused on getting a shot of the bit where Kim's long legs met and ignored Nathan and the bodyguard who made an exit out of the door in the other side of the hoverer.

Well, they didn't ignore them completely but by the time they noticed Nathan he was already inside the studio building.

The next hour and a half were used in perfecting his appearance, and then he was escorted to David Moss' Blue Room by a runner robot.

The other guests were already waiting.

The Blue Room was filled to the brim with booze and nondescript little packs that Nathan guessed contained little something to keep those guests satisfied who didn't worry about the legality of substances available.

Derrick Moore, a famous Peking film actor who had made a career out of playing American villains in Chinese dramas, over sixty but looking barely thirty, was already working his way through the bottles, secure in the knowledge that if his liver packed up he could always get a new one.

Yanita, the 23-year old MarsGritTweetPop sensation with an ambiguous ethnic identity sat next to Derrick. She had hit the top spot in the Galaxy Charts three weeks ago, and still occupied it, which in the music business was an eternity.

David Moss walked in the studio around half an hour later, and by this time Derrick was clearly drunk. He was the first guest, and he almost fell when he stumbled on to the sofa to be interviewed. He was dressed in his trademark space cowboy boots, torn jeans and blue blazer. The studio crowd erupted in applauds and cheers when they saw him. He leaned on the sofa in an exaggeratedly relaxed pose.

"Nice to have you here!"

"Nice place! Where are we?"

"London, Planet Earth. Let's talk about your new hybrid film."

Derrick might have been drunk but he could do the promotional work half-asleep, and, in any case, any slur or stumbling could be masked even in a live show, and this was a recorded show, which gave a lot more scope to fix any flaws in performance.

"As most people know, we don't act all the scenarios. There are an infinite number of potential endings. But in any case, most viewers want to end the story with me in the bar, after I've shot all the villains. That's the storyline we always focus on."

David Moss ran through Derrick's career, first as a villain in Hong Kong holo-games, then as a character actor in old-fashioned singular story films, and now as a Peking superstar.

"It has been hell of a ride! Three hundred and twenty-seven roles in films and games, five wives and seventeen kids."

"And that's just the kids and wives people know about!"

The studio audience burst into laughter.

"Let's talk about your latest game, *The Galaxy Quest*. A bunch of actors play star travellers who are invited by aliens to save them from extinction. I played it last week, and it certainly has a great sense of adventure. The third level seems pretty much impenetrable. Can you give us any tips?"

"The only character who actually can survive the level is McGyver."

"Some players have actually died during the gameplay. Do you feel responsible?"

"That just makes it more exciting."

"Let's talk about your new religion. You are rumoured to have left behind your wild days. What is Canis Major about?"

"Canis Major, formerly known as Jack Smith received a revelation about the galaxy of Canis Manor as the location of the ultimate reality, heaven, nirvana, or whatever you want to call it."

"Canis Major is about twenty-five thousand light years from us. How will you get there?"

"At an appointed time a wormhole will open up. He and his followers will be in the Earth's end of the wormhole, waiting."

"How will this wormhole you believe in form?"

"Aliens, or gods have told Canis Manor about the creation of that wormhole. They will also reveal to him its location and the exact time when it will open up."

"What is your heaven like?"

"The atmosphere of the planets in Canis Manor is optimal for human existence. It will lengthen the human life span so that anyone can live thousands of years. With anti-age treatment, we could be talking about life that is practically eternal. And who wouldn't want to live eternally?" Derrick asked, now looking at the studio audience.

"And how will you get through the wormhole?"

"We are raising money and building a needle ship that has seats for 144,000 disciples of Canis Manor."

"How can one get a seat?"

"They don't come cheap. Also, you need to actually convert to the religion."

After Derrick it was Nathan's turn. His legs weighed a ton, like a mining robot's legs, as he left the Blue Room and entered the studio. The studio audience stood up and began to clap spontaneously when David Moss announced his arrival.

"Neeta sends her thanks. Unfortunately, she can't be here tonight," David Moss said.

The guest sofa wasn't nearly as comfortable as it looked. Also, David Moss was a lot tinier figure than he had expected, and he wore high heels to disguise his tininess.

Yet, he had survived the many culls in the industry, and nearly always run a top show, so there had to be plenty of steel inside the feeble-looking frame.

"What went through your mind straight after the explosion?"

"I didn't have time to think."

"Why did you go back to the carriage?"

"I don't know. I just had a strange feeling. That someone might still be alive."

"That must have taken a lot of courage."

"The worst thing was the darkness. The real danger was already over."

"Your cousin died in that same carriage. How have you coped with that?"

"Thankfully, I didn't know that she was there."

"I have spoken to your father in many occasions. He is a wonderful man. Great to see that the son is made of the same titanium!"

His bit was over as abruptly as it had begun. He stayed in the Blue Room to the end of the program and watched David talk to Yanita.

"What is MarsGritTweetPop?" David asked.

"MarsGritTweetPop combines the rhythms of the Red Planet with the ancient beats of Grit, Tweet and Pop. It was created by the Afro-German miners who first mined the planet. It all began from drumming the steel cage of the lift."

"All good music is the end result of boredom. Or despair. Have you ever been to Mars?"

"Dad was a miner. I was born there."

Nathan's robot minders stood outside the Blue Room, waiting. Their task was to make sure that Nathan's interview remained exclusive. He was escorted to a hoverer and taken to Hotel Asparagus.

"You can go to the nightclub but you can't leave the building. The place is secure."

After two hours in his hotel room, his wrist pad disconnected, the advice of the robot minder about visiting the nightclub began to sound reasonable. He headed to the bar downstairs, and could hear the live band play jazz when he got out of the lift.

Hotel Asparagus was a galaxy-level operation that could afford a word-class human jazz band play in a half-empty bar. Nathan sat down, ordered a Pina Neptunus, stared at the wall, and let the music carry him away.

"Nathan!"

He turned around to see Yanita.

"I can't sleep either," she said. "Although I really should, as I will be flying to New Tokyo in the morning."

"Last time I was there, I was taken to a place that served live octopus."

"I never get to see any of the exciting places. Apart from going to the gig venue I hardly leave the hotel room."

"Do you want to dance?" she asked after finishing her drink.

"Not really."

"Come on! This place is so boring." She didn't wait for an

answer but took hold of his hand and pulled him off the bar stool. The pianist smiled when he saw them taking the first dance steps.

At least he would get some job satisfaction.

She was a good dancer. She smelled good. She pulled him closer. When the song ended she let go of him. Perhaps she had realised that he wasn't a lot of fun.

"I really need to go to bed now. Would you kindly escort me to my room?"

There was no point in objecting, as she was already pulling him across the room.

Yanita's room was on the seventh floor. It looked like a presidential suite. When they got in, a gigantic AllNet screen came on and started playing Yanita's song.

She seemed to like her own music.

"Please wait," she said. "These hotels are so lonely. All you see is robot servants."

She opened the door to the bathroom.

"I'll order some drinks," she said. "But I need to change first."

Nathan sat on a chair and leaned back. At least there would be someone to talk to.

The room's walls that had looked like they had been painted in black suddenly became a waterfall, and the atmosphere was filled with tropic scents and singing of birds.

Then Yanita came out. First it seemed that she wore nothing but then the transparent dress she wore started to glitter with the colours of the rainbow.

She danced solo in front of him, the rainbow colours playing on her body. Her eyes gleamed like sapphires. It was clear that she had taken some DY-21, and that she would be ready to sleep with anything that moved or had a little bit of life left in it.

He stood up, and embraced her, instinctively. After all, that was what you were supposed to do to a beautiful, practically naked woman.

He kissed her on the lips. They smelled of wine. She closed her eyes.

"I can't do this," he said abruptly.

When she opened her eyes their hazy softness was gone.

"What's wrong with you?"

"Sorry. This has nothing to do with you."

"So you fancy robot boys!"

"No. There is someone else."

By now her dress had lost all its transparency.

Nathan left the room without saying goodbye, took the lift to his floor, and packed his gym bag. It was 3.09am. He took the lift down but got out on the 1st floor. Then he walked down the stairs but rather than going past the robot receptionist, he waited until he saw a human porter, a young man who wore an old-fashioned red uniform you could only see in luxury hotels.

"Could you please let me out by the back door? I'm trying to avoid the paparazzi."

He was also trying to avoid his minders that might still be in the lobby, or outside, but that was information the young man didn't need to know. The porter seemed happy to oblige, seemingly accustomed to these kinds of requests, and Nathan authorised a hefty tip before he slipped out.

Ten years ago Nathan would have slept with the pin-up girl of the moment with gratefulness and savoured it.

But it had all changed in the monastery.

Strange how he could trace so many new things and attitudes in his life to the few months he had spent in the Japanese monastery, and more specifically to the moment he had taken his wrist pad off for the first time.

It was a well-known fact that wrist pads enhanced positive emotions and suppressed negative ones, making each moment and experience somewhat more exciting that they would have been without it, and reducing the level of aggression in most people.

Wearing wrist pads made sex sexier and the smoky flavour of smoked ham even smokier.

That's why most scientists recommended wearing them.

How could anything that reduced murder rate and suicides be bad for society?

The wrist pads also made the cheap food created in the lab more palatable than it really was.

He had once taken his wrist pad off in an Oxford restaurant to discover that their normally tasty curry in fact had quite chemical and disgusting flavour. He had not been there ever since.

He had been cooking using natural and organic ingredients after that. He knew that not everyone could afford it.

He could.

He walked to Lola's apartment. According to the wrist pad, it would take him two hours to walk to Lola's, and it was strongly discouraging him from doing that and taking a taxi instead.

He had to clear his head.

He wore a hooded top to ward off any instant recognition. It didn't really matter, as streets were empty of people and traffic.

It was 5.15am when Nathan climbed up the shrieking stairs. When he opened the door he was greeted by a welcoming mix of scents made of Lola's perfume, home-cooked food, and the other smells only a woman's presence can create.

Lola was fast asleep. He lay down on the sofa, pulled a blanket over and fell asleep.

When he woke up, the breakfast was ready. She stood by the door in cute flowery pyjamas, smiled irresistibly, and if there ever had been any regret in Nathan's mind about not sleeping with Yanita, it left him.

After Lola left to work, Nathan fell asleep on her bed.

It was 2.32pm when he woke up. He pulled the curtains open to let the sunlight in, and out of the habit he had developed only recently, he scanned the street level. The street looked quiet.

Only a few hoverers were parked outside. He could see a black

Mercedes opposite the front door with two men inside. It was an expensive model, and its spotlessly clean and shining roof reflected the contours of building on the opposite side.

The window was open, and an African man's hand hang out. It held a cigarette.

Most definitely, they weren't reporters. The driver looked up, noticed him, and dropped his cigarette on the street. He shut the window, and the hoverer took off. Nathan watched it float along the street, and turn around the corner.

What were they doing there?

That seemed odd but maybe it was just a coincidence.

21.

Three days later the story about his heroism was dead. It had peaked seventeen hours after the first interview had been broadcast and then receded. Duncan could now be discharged, and Nathan's life returned to normal. Still, his short-lived fame seemed to have a lasting impact on his kudos in the academic world. The lecture room that had originally been booked for his series on the African circles turned out to be far too small, as over four hundred students had signed up.

The school's largest auditorium was overcrowded, with students sitting on stairs, and it was bubbling with chatter and excitement when he walked in.

The chatter ended abruptly when the students saw him. He walked to the lectern.

"So you're all here to learn about the world's oldest circles. That's a minor miracle in itself! But lets get straight to the topic. What comes to your mind when you hear the word 'Outworld'?"

"Poverty and disease," an English-looking young girl in the front row quipped.

"The Wall," someone else shouted.

Thirty-five years ago, the Solar Nations had erected a fifty-foot high wall that separated Northern Africa from the rest of the continent.

The Wall existed to control immigration from the densely populated black African nations, but it kept Africa's Mediterranean coast, its holiday resorts, villas and the pyramids accessible to the Europeans.

"Today, we try to keep the Africans out, but the continent hasn't always been poor. Some of the world's greatest empires and civilisations were built there. The first ever star cruiser is about to depart to 55 Cancri, and the future of humanity lies outside this solar system. Yet, without Africa, there would be no humanity, language, civilisation, or even religion."

Nathan sipped water from the glass the robot caretaker had brought to him.

"Ethiopia is the cradle of humanity. The oldest human fossils, around two million years old, have all been found in Ethiopia. All humans alive today can be traced back to a small tribe of hunter-gatherers who lived in Africa sixty thousand years ago. We are all Africans, regardless of our race."

At least the front row seemed to still be listening. "But this series isn't about the evolution of humanity but about the history of religion." He paused.

"My hypothesis is that the first religion originated in Africa," he continued. "Contrary to what many people believe religion matters today. In the beginning of every century people proclaim the end of it, but so far, it has refused to die. Maybe it is all based on a mutation in our brain, a mutation that was helpful in the past. Whatever the reason, it seems to be part of our DNA. It might be an illusion but it is a lasting one. And it seems that it began with star-gazing and it might not end just because we are now reaching the stars. Consider this. The first human structure erected in Mars was a titanium circle, erected by the Order."

Some students in the audience burst into laughter.

"This leads us conveniently to the circles in Africa. Does anyone know where the British stone circles come from?"

A few students raised their hands. Nathan pointed at the blonde girl in the third row.

"The first stone circles were erected on the British Isles

thousands of years ago," she said. "The Order claims that they are a British invention yet critical research has proved that they might have come from the Continent."

"Good. That is what we have known up to today. My hypothesis is that the first stone circles, which are also some of the first constructions with religious significance were in fact erected in the desert of Sahara. We have discovered the Earth's oldest astronomical stone circle alignments in Nabta Playa. They are at least six thousand and five hundred years old and at least thousand years older than the British equivalents.

"So what? That doesn't prove anything!" exclaimed the young man from the audience. It was clear that he held pro-Order views.

"It might. Let's move on to our research site in Nabta Playa." The 3D projector showed a partially dug research site in the middle of the desert. There were twenty-four stone slabs, around half of the nine feet of the stones above the ground level. They formed a circle.

"How do you know that this is a religious construction?" someone asked.

"We'll get to that," Nathan said. "First, let's look at the topography of the area around six thousand years ago."

The 3D projector showed a shoreline of a lake.

"This is Sahara as it used to be. As you can see, it hasn't always been a desert. Let's zoom in here."

By the shore, there were the remains of a stone circle.

"We have so far discovered five of them, each only a short distance from the lake. Now, let's look at the lake five and half thousand years ago."

The shoreline had now receded and was about a half a mile away from the location of the stone circles.

"Around six thousand years ago, the ancient lake would have sustained a large population. Now, the whole area is hyperacid and uninhabitable. The erosion process would have been slow, taking hundreds if not thousands of years. I believe that the stone circles were erected to stop the erosion of the lake. They were religious constructions, built to plead the gods to reverse the curse of drought."

"Maybe they were fishing huts," someone objected.

"That would be the first time when fishing huts have some astrological significance."

"How can we know that?" The question came from the young man who had been yawning before. At least, he had now woken up.

"Good thing you asked. In the centre of the stone circle that we spent most of our time with is a sculptured rock that resembles a cow standing upright. As you might know, the cow goddesses were popular in Egypt. Interestingly, the Egyptians themselves attested the African origin of many of their gods and goddesses. But lest this wasn't enough, there is more."

He paused. He seemed to have everyone's attention.

"The circles are astrological constructions, built thousands of years before the Sumerians and Babylonians, the 'fathers' of astrology, invented their craft. The stone circles points exactly towards the horizon of the summer solstice. We are looking at the first star gates, the oldest surviving astrological structures on Earth. It seems that whoever built them knew astrology."

It was now completely quiet in the auditorium.

"Who constructed them? What was their significance? Whatever the answers are, it is an indisputable fact that six and half thousand years ago and thousands of years before the Sumerians and Egyptians, a group of people understood astrology in the Nubian Desert."

The silence had now become audible.

"The site where we spent most of the nine months is known as Nabta, and consists of a stone circle, a series of flat, tomb-like stone structures and five lines of standing and toppled megaliths. Located west of the Nile River in southern Egypt, Nabta predates

Stonehenge and similar prehistoric sites around the world by over thousand years. As far as we know, it is the first stone circle in the world."

A young man in the fifth row seemed distressed. Perhaps the air-conditioning wasn't working there nearly as well as on the stage. The building was old and not all the equipment functioned perfectly.

"The ruins lie on the shoreline of an ancient lake that began filling with water about eleven thousand years ago when the African summer monsoon shifted north. It was used by nomads until about five thousand and two hundred years ago, when the monsoon moved southwest and the area again became hyper-arid and uninhabitable. No human remains have been found yet at Nabta, but remains of cattle can be seen. Based on the results of our expedition, many archaeologists and others believe the complex and symbolic Nabta culture may have stimulated the growth of the society that eventually constructed the first pyramids along the Nile about four thousand and five hundred years ago."

A man in the back lifted his arm.

"If Africans built the first stone circles could they also have invented the religion of the druids here in Britain? Surely the fact that they both have stone circles cannot be a coincidence?"

Nathan thought for a moment before replying. The question must have been on everyone's lips.

"It is difficult and perhaps impossible to prove a causal relationship between the erection of the stone circles in Africa and Britain around a thousand years later. But obviously building stone circles is certainly such a rare occurrence in the world that it certainly points to that direction. But some important work needs to be done before we can establish that conclusively."

"Blasphemy!" The young man that had earlier seemed agitated stood up. He pulled a small pistol from his pocket and before Nathan had time to react he started shooting. Fortunately, his aim wasn't that good and the bullets hit the lectern and the screen behind him.

The students sitting between him and the shooter hid under the seats.

Nathan dived behind the lectern. The audience started screaming and headed towards the emergency exits. The young man jumped over the row of seats and leaped toward him.

Now he stood around ten feet away, close enough to hit the target.

He lifted the gun and pointed at him. "Die, you heretic scumbag!" he screamed.

Nathan closed his eyes and waited for the bullet to hit him, hoping that the resuscitating robots would turn up before he was completely brain-dead.

The shot never came. When he opened his eyes he saw the young man on the floor, held by two security robots.

Jack stood in front of them.

"I knew that your visit would bring the university much-needed publicity," he said. "Just didn't know how much."

The security robots dragged the attacker out of the auditorium.

"Next time, we need to screen the students," Jack said.

22.

The backlash came swiftly, although the AllNet media still generally framed him as a hero. Without the attacker raising the stakes because of the media coverage that followed it, the issue of the allegedly African origin of the stone circles would have remained strictly academic.

Now the story hit the national and international headlines.

In an attempt to explain the raison d'être behind the attack and make it interesting the media greatly oversimplified the story. It became a story about the heroic albeit rebellious son of the chief druid intent on bringing the Order down.

Dad seemed to take it all relatively calmly.

After fifteent angry calls, and some menacing, borderline death threats, Nathan blocked all the calls from anyone but friends. It seemed that there were many people living in Britain that felt as strongly about the allegedly divine British origins of the Order as the attacker.

The attacker was a twenty-five-year-old student named Jim Strugger, a member of the Order, not a professional hit man, fortunately, but someone who had nevertheless managed to get hold of an un-licensed gun, not that it was difficult. The media portrayed him as a deranged loner with the past of being bullied.

This time around, after having found Nathan a fairly boring interviewee, the studios were packed with anti-Order guests debating with the representatives of the Order about the alleged dangers of the druidic religion, mostly in a heated contest but occasionally in a rather civilised debate.

For Duncan, the most important issue was to portray the Order as a tolerant organisation, capable of dealing with criticism in a mature way, and Jim Strugger as a lunatic.

The Order didn't produce religious fundamentalists.

Whoever had nailed the dead rabbit on Nathan's front door must have remained unconvinced of the tolerant nature of the Order.

Apart from scrubbing the bloody remains of the rabbit from the front door and waiting for the suspended lectures in the School of African Studies to restart after improved security screenings, a fix easily funded by the influx of new donations that had now started to come in, Nathan laid low, working on the translation of the texts found in Ethiopia and waiting for the media storm to subside.

One and half weeks later when the lectures were about to begin again Nathan finally packed a gym bag and headed to London.

It was Tuesday afternoon, and his intention was to make it to Lola's workplace before the end of her shift to surprise her. She could always give her a lift in the scooter, as she had a spare helmet. Nathan wasn't a keen scooterer but the average speeds in London were fairly low, and the short journey would be bearable.

It was 5.25pm. He rushed up the escalator ofTottenham Court Road underground station, the nearest station to Lola's office. He navigated through the crowds of Oxford Street and made it to a side alley that led to her office.

He was running late. He could see Lola come out and get on top of the scooter. He was about to shout but his voice got stuck in the throat when he saw a black Mercedes like the one that had been parked in front of Lola's house only weeks earlier.

He slowed down. The windows of the hoverer were darkened

but he could see a black man's arm holding a cigarette hanging from the open side window.

That man smoked a lot.

He hid in an entrance to a shop, and watched the situation develop.

He wanted to see if they would follow Lola. He could always take the train and beat them to Lola's house as the street-level traffic moved slower than the trains.

Lola slipped into the traffic. The driver of the black hoverer waited until there were three hoverers between before he followed her. Now he was certain that they were after her.

Usually Lola headed straight back to her place. He tried to call her but her wrist pad was switched off.

He forced himself to calm down as he sat in the train. Perhaps the men were simply monitoring her, although the reason why they might have done that escaped his imagination.

Fifteen minutes later, he came out of Holland Park underground station, and started running. The evening sunshine was still hot enough to make him sweat, and the back of his shirt was soaking within seconds. But now wasn't the time to worry about personal hygiene.

He wasn't a superhero but right now he wished to become one. He slowed his pace when he turned around the corner to Lola's street.

There was no sign of Lola or the black Mercedes yet. He sat on the stairs around six doors away from Lola's front door.

A few minutes later Lola's scooter approached. She parked it by the pavement and pulled out her grocery shopping from the storage trunk.

The black Mercedes had by now parked a few doors down the street and the two black men came out. They walked toward Lola. It seemed clear that she didn't know them, as she didn't react to their proximity.

The men looked like they were about to pass her but they

didn't. When she opened the front door, they jumped up the stairs and forced her in.

The front door closed behind. It had all happened so quickly that had he not been watching them closely he would have missed it all.

These men moved like professional thugs.

They had looked rather muscular, and he had been close enough to notice that they sported ugly-looking tribal scars on their faces. That told him they had been born and raised in an African village in the Outworld rather than the British Isles.

Their hoverer looked expensive. Lola had never told him about her husband but he concluded that these men might have something to do with him or his family rather than whatever trouble she might have been in over here in London.

He had no idea about what weapons the men might be carrying. The only one he had was the element of surprise. These two men wouldn't expect a university lecturer half their size to be dangerous.

He ran fast. He had to get in before the men made it to Lola's flat, as the security system would alert them to his entry if they were already in the apartment. He opened the door and got in.

He could hear noises up in the staircase, and he waited until he heard them quieten. It seemed that the men wanted to get inside her apartment, and it was better that they would get into cleaning the place of valuables or whatever they were planning to do before he would get in so that their attention would be fixed on that. He doubted that the men were out to rape her, or to kill; they could have put that kind of plan to action weeks ago.

The wooden planks under the red carpet shrieked loud under his steps and he felt the wild palpitation of his heart.

He pressed an ear to the door and could hear muffled talk. He had no idea about where the men were in the apartment but he hoped that they wouldn't be in the reception hall.

He pulled the door open quietly and peeked in.

There was no one in the hall.

He slid in and closed the door behind.

The conversation between the two men came from the front room. Nathan sneaked in to the kitchen and picked a knife from the rack, sliding it under the belt. It would provide emergency protection if the situation would turn really nasty.

Thank gods none of the household robots reacted to his arrival. One of them stood by the kitchen door, clearly alarmed about what was taking place in the front room but unable to do anything.

He stepped in to the front room.

The larger man held Lola whilst the slightly smaller man was busy stuffing a large gym bag with the Yoruba jewellery from the mantelpiece.

"What's going on?" Nathan asked.

The men turned towards him and the surprise on their faces swiftly turned to bloodlust.

"If you run now, we might let you live," the smaller man stuffing the bag said.

"It's you who will leave," Nathan said.

"Hey, the white midget thinks he's got superpowers," he responded.

"Run now! Before it's too late!" Lola screamed.

"I'm not going anywhere until these two retards are gone," Nathan said.

"I'll cut your balls off!"

The man dropped his bag on the floor in rage and pulled out a nasty-looking machete.

Man could draw brute power from rage but if he did, his precision and ability to calculate rationally worsened.

Nathan rather fought against a raging man than a calm one and did his best to enrage his opponents.

"Be careful not to cut your fingers, you monkey," he said to the smaller man with the machete.

"First, I'll cut your balls off and then I will feed them to you. Then, I'll watch you bleed to death."

He could see genuine horror on Lola's face and remembered that she had never seen him fighting.

At close look these men looked more like muscles without brain rather than intelligent fighters.

Aikido was Japanese and signified 'the way of spiritual harmony'. He had never utilised its twisting and throwing techniques that turned the attacker's strength and momentum against himself in a battle with an opponent intent to kill but he had practised *sankyo*, the art of stripping the opponent off his knife hundreds of times. It made no difference that the man was twice as large as him; with *sankyo*, a child could disarm the world's strongest man.

Or so went the theory.

The man stepped toward him, rotating the machete with his fingers, an act designed to demonstrate his skill but also a sign of arrogant nervousness that would only slow him down a split second, as part of his mind would be focused on the rolling blade.

"Come to your butcher!"

He took one more step toward Nathan.

Nathan leaped forward. The blade missed his arm narrowly as the man plunged. He took hold of the machete-holding hand and twisted it. Then he pushed it backwards and stepped sideways. The man tried to kick him. Nathan twisted his arm toward his body.

The man screamed of pain. Nathan twisted harder until he heard the snapping of a breaking bone. The machete dropped on the floor. The man followed.

Nathan picked the machete from the floor and threw it out of the way.

Aikido was a defensive sport with no attacking moves, and Nathan's trainer had always encouraged him to mix it with karate, the art of the 'empty hand' that incorporated offensive moves to its repertoire, an unorthodox approach that could save your life if you faced a street fight.

Nathan opted for palm heel strike. Tucking in his thumbs and tightening his wrist, he thrust his palm toward the second man that was now plunging toward him, striking with the heel of his palm, with his fingers pointing upward and the heel of the palm forward, like he had practised thousands of times.

His mind was free of rage when his palm hit the man who fell on the floor.

The palm heel strike was a move that could kill but Nathan had limited the impact. There was no need to kill a man and have the police come around. It would only complicate things.

"The police will be here shortly," Nathan said.

"We'll deal with you later," the smaller man growled as they stumbled out.

Nathan watched from the window as they got in their hoverer and left.

He put his arms around Lola. She was shaking.

"Do you know them?"

"Not personally. But I know they were sent by my ex-husband to abduct me. He doesn't believe in divorce."

Her eyes had never seemed as pained.

"I have never told you about my ex-husband."

"I don't need to know."

They drank green tea in the kitchen.

Her anxiety had lifted but she seemed shaken about the fact that some shadows from her past had come to get her.

Nathan searched through the bag the thugs had left behind. It was a disposable black polyester bag that could have been bought from anywhere.

There was nothing to give away their identity.

Lola didn't want to talk to the police either.

"My ex-husband knows some powerful people. There is no

need to arouse his anger even further by taking this to the police."

"Why don't we go to Oxford tonight?" Nathan asked. "It would be good to create some distance between us and tonight's events."

"Let's do that."

Half an hour later they were out. They headed to King's Circle and caught a city hopper that flew them through not-so-dark night sky to Oxford. It landed at the central station and Nathan hailed a taxi to take them to his house. He had already warned Edgar who had cooked a Thai meal and lit up the wood in the fireplace.

Then he went to have a shower. When he came back she was clearing the dishes from the table.

"Edgar will do it. Just leave them."

"I find washing the dishes relaxing." She continued piling the dishes in the sink. Nathan had a brush and washing liquid, and she found them. She began to scrub the plates.

"I had to do that in Sahara. That's why I got the brush."

Her curves shone through the slightly transparent fabric of the flowery dress. He put his arms around her and pulled her closer.

"Are you sure you're fine?" he asked, trying to keep his voice steady, as the scent of her perfume and body began to intoxicate him.

"I'm OK," she said, her voice slightly hoarser than usual. She let him hold her without resistance, and he felt the softness of her flesh under the skirt.

"Nathan. I have always liked you a lot," she said. "But you are always so busy travelling the world that you pay no notice to me."

And he had kept the distance as he thought she wasn't interested.

He kissed her neck, the scent of the coconut lotion on her body making him drunk.

He let his hands climb up to her breasts. Her nipples hardened under his caressing fingers.

"I fear losing you from my life," he said. "I'd rather have you as a friend than as an ex."

"I'd rather have you as en ex than a man who never took his chances."

They stood there, two bodies merging into one; with the corner of his eye Nathan could see Edgar flick its lights for approval before leaving the room.

"Give me fifteen minutes," she said. "After that, come to get me."

She left the kitchen and he could hear her steps in the stairs.

Nathan paced around the kitchen restlessly for the next fourteen and a half minutes and then he started to climb up the stairs.

He found her on top floor, in the meditation room.

She sat on the tatami that the simulator had converted into a beach with a Hawaiian sunset as a backdrop. She wore a hula skirt, her brown body glowing in the evening sun.

"How do you switch this machine off?"

"Unless you override it manually it sets a landscape that it deems appropriate for your desired state of mind."

The Hawaiian setting disappeared, which left Lola sitting on the tatami in an empty room. She was dressed in her semi-transparent nightgown.

"And take your wrist pad away," she said. "I want to feel you, in all your imperfection, rather than an idealised version of you."

Nathan removed his wrist pad and placed it on the floor. Then he took all his clothes off, and for a moment, he just stood there, naked.

Then he sat down on the floor and put his arms around her. He kissed her lips, first clumsily and the softly.

Afterwards, it dawned on him that he had never made love. He had always had sex. There was a vast ocean between the smoothed simulator-facilitated sex that tried hard to be better than the real thing, and the real thing.

Making love made you feel vulnerable, imperfect, a little bit dirty due to all the liquid involved but at least for a fleeting moment *one* with the one you made love to.

It removed the invisible electronic shield that separated people from each other and forced them to face their real selves.

For the first time he understood the histories about men who had fought kingdoms to win the love of a woman. He lay on the tatami, stared at the moon, and smiled. He couldn't remember when it was the last time he had been this happy.

The book that Nathan was reading, *The Unofficial History of the McKinley Clan*, traced the origins of his family to Edinburgh, Scotland. The first druids of any prominence in his family had appeared around eight hundred and fifty years ago in the Scottish Highlands.

"Any luck?"

Sam had appeared next to him without him noticing his arrival, so focused had he been on the contents of the book.

"It is all very interesting. But I'm not sure what is fact and what fiction."

When he had requested Sam for access to whatever material the Old British Library held for their family, and especially offline, he hadn't divulged in the details of why he was looking for something.

He had deliberately avoided any books that were connected to the AllNet.

If Morris Chapman's theory had any foundation in reality then someone would be monitoring their use.

"Let me know if you find anything interesting."

The first few hundred years had been hardly noteworthy. It was only when the family had moved to Oxford around six hundred and fifty years ago that it had achieved any prominence.

Nine hours later, when he had finished reading the family history he had a feeling that Morris Chapman could well be right.

There had been three hundred and seventeen unnatural deaths in the last eight hundred years.

Eighty-seven of them seemed odd and their aftermath even stranger.

Some of them really stood out.

Three hundred and fifty-two years ago, Erica, a daughter of John McKinley, an army colonel, had been raped and stabbed over fifty times.

Six months later John McKinley had been made into a general, rather inexplicably, as it was the time for hundred-year peace.

Two hundred and fifty-seven years ago, Peter McKinley, an influential trader of cotton, coffee, tea and other luxury goods had tragically lost his wife.

He had lost her or she had vanished.

According to some she had run away with a black servant but then the servant's dismembered body had been found in a ditch two weeks later.

Three months later, Peter McKinley had got an exclusive right to import cotton from India.

Eighty-seven years ago, Winston McKinley's daughter, Evelyn, had been run over by a train. She had been identified through a DNA sample.

Three months later, Winston, an MP with relatively low stature, had become the youngest ever Chancellor of the Exchequer.

If there was a pattern it seemed to be a tragedy followed by an unexpected kick of fortune.

Bear mauls a Highland girl.

The news headline about Eleanor's gruesome death wasn't extraordinary in itself. What made it extraordinary was that bears were thought to have had been extinct on the British Isles for hundreds of years.

Oxfordshire Reaper strikes again.

The Reaper, never caught alive, had been linked to brutal murders of twenty-eight women, eight of whom had been McKinleys.

The Reaper had never confessed as he had been gunned down after a siege. The evidence for killings had been discovered in his apartment, including the personal possessions of twenty-three victims.

So far, he had counted fifteen female members of the family who had vanished without a trace and who had never been found.

These excluded the deaths after the Do-Muzude.

Eight clear murders.

Five women who were still missing.

Seven accidents, some suspicious, such as the death of his distant cousin in a hovering accident.

Mum and Guinevere.

History seemed to prove that McKinleys had some very unlucky family members. He had never studied the history of any other families so he didn't have a benchmark to compare with but there seemed to be disproportionate amount of misfortune in the family.

On the other hand, there had also been disproportionate amount of luck.

The rest of McKinleys, the ones who hadn't lost their lives through murder or freak accidents, or who hadn't just vanished, had become very successful people.

Nathan got up and an archiving robot came to pick the books he had left on the table.

23.

Nathan observed as two security robots scanned the students dribbling in through the lecture room door and checked their identities and pockets.

The school wasn't taking any risks this time.

There were fewer students but the remaining ones would at least be genuinely interested in the actual subject.

Nathan took his jacket off; even with the air-conditioning in full power the room still felt stifling.

"We will move on from the origin of the stone circles to less dangerous aspects of African history."

Some students laughed, first nervously then in a relaxed manner, and then someone started clapping.

Suddenly, the whole auditorium stood up and gave him a standing ovation.

Nathan waited until the students had taken their seats and the noise had receded.

"Around six months ago, I came across a copy of a document that had been buried in the archives of the Old British Library for over one hundred years. The original was written in the kingdom of Aksum almost two thousand years ago. But let's not move foward so quickly. Who knows anything about Aksum?"

Two students raised their hands.

"It was an African kingdom during the Antiquity," the brunette tried.

"Pretty good! On scale, can you tell me how large or powerful the kingdom was?"

"It was about twice the size of the modern Ethiopia," the girl responded.

"Not bad. But did you know that according to the writers of the Antiquity, Aksum was one of the world's four powerful empires, competing with Rome, China and Persia? It had one of the highest literacy rates in the ancient world. It minted its own coins and had monumental architecture. Yet today, less than 0.01 per cent of the world's population has heard about it. The history of Aksum is one of the Earth's great mysteries."

Nathan glanced around the lecture hall to see if the students were still focused on the lecture.

Most of them seemed still to be there.

"Over the last five months, I have spent most of my time attempting to translate a book written in early Geez. The book was ransacked by the British army from Ethiopia around two hundred and fifty years ago. It contains four renditions of a story about a spiritual master, told from four slightly different perspectives. His identity remains a mystery. There are no references to him beyond these four texts, and not a single mention about him in the whole canon of Geez literature. You might ask whether these texts refer to a real or fictional character, and admittedly, there can't be hundred per cent assurance whether the spiritual teacher ever lived or if he was the figment of someone's religious imagination. 'Who cares?' you might ask."

A handful of students burst to laughter.

"We have a religious revolutionary, a real or invented one, who appears to have made a unique contribution to religious thought. Yet we have never heard of him. Why didn't his religion take off but why did Buddha's? That's one of the questions I am attempting to answer."

"But does any of it matter today?" someone asked. "Both Buddha and the teacher are dead."

"The past affects the future and the future affects the past due to the relativity of time. All time flows simultaneously, so even my thoughts about the past can theoretically affect it."

"What has this to do with McClauden's theorem of time?" the young man who had asked the first question responded.

"Everything has something to do with McClauden's theorem of time."

After the lecture he spoke with the students that stayed behind to ask questions. Jack had come in the lecture room in the end of the lecture and he sat in the front row, waiting for him to finish.

"What's up, Jack?" Nathan asked after the last student left.

"It's time for us to have a drink and celebrate! In the last two months our donations have increased by one thousand five hundred per cent. On the minus side, the Order has withdrawn their grant but that has always been a token number." He grinned broadly. "Due to the publicity caused by the attack during your lecture, our financial problems have become the past."

After the drinks Nathan took an evening hopper to Oxford. He had already had his supper when the doorbell rang.

A wrinkled face of Neftalem, the Eritrean librarian from the Old British Library, filled the screen. The white, balding hair and the skin starved of moisturiser combined with bright eyes that looked half his age reminded him of the Japanese monks he had met at the temple—men of spirit rather than war. Neftalem had always been an enigma to him; there seemed to be deep intelligence beneath his skin and yet he had worked in a lowly position at the library for decades.

"Is that Nathan McKinley?"

"Yes it is. What brings you here?"

"I have something very important I need to share with you. It can't wait."

He had no idea why Neftalem would be here just before midnight but he didn't come across as someone who would spend his nights wasting everyone's time.

When Neftalem got in he looked tinier and frailer than before. He had lost weight.

"Do you want anything to drink? I have some Ethiopian coffee I brought from the Outworld."

"I'd love a cup."

Edgar's ears were always open even when it wasn't in the room and moments later it appeared holding a singular cup of steaming coffee on a silver tray.

"That's great! Reminds me of home! And the taste is perfect," Naftalem said after he had slurped the coffee.

"Edgar must be the best barista in the world."

"I didn't tell you that my ancestors were the guardians of the book."

"What book?"

"The book you are translating. But at the time there was no need to share that information."

"It doesn't seem your ancestors did a good job, considering that it was lost in the Old British Library for over two hundred and fifty years."

"And where do you think the guardians have been for the last two hundred and fifty years?"

"Why didn't you find a way to take it back?"

"The book has no value as a physical object. It is the content that interests us. And it doesn't mean that we can understand its message just because we are Ethiopians. The early Geez is a dead language and for over one thousand years no one has been able to read it."

"How did the book end up with the Emperor Tewodoros?"

"He ransacked the monasteries for gold but didn't value the books. He kept them as he knew he could blackmail the monasteries. My ancestor Tobalus was in the fortress when the British army attacked the fortress. He was wounded but he survived. When the British archaeologist who travelled with the army took the book it became the task of his son Arbulus to get it back. He travelled to London. It soon became evident to him that the library where the book ended up might be the safest place to keep it. No one knew what it was and the Abyssinian power battles couldn't touch it there. So, Arbulus got a job as a curator in the museum due to his knowledge of Geez. And after that, one of the guardians has always worked for the library. Until now. Our wait is now over."

"As the book is now back in Ethiopia."

"Not quite. We haven't been waiting for that."

"I thought this was all about the book."

"As I said it has never been about the book as a physical object."

"Why haven't your tried to translate it yourself?"

"The job isn't that easy. The seers used to say that the meaning was lost because the world wasn't judged ready for the message."

"Why not?"

"The message could become a blessing or a curse. That's why the content would be locked until an interpreter would come. The coming of the interpreter would signal the new era of understanding and the world would receive the message rather than reject it."

"And who or what is the interpreter?"

"We believe it is you."

"You must be mistaken. I only have an academic interest. I am not interested in the spiritual message of the book. Apart from my interest in the early Geez language and learning more about the kingdom of Aksum, this book doesn't seem beneficial to me. And it has probably never been originally written in Geez which compromises my quest to understand the culture of Aksum. I don't think the book will reveal to us anything about the ancient African culture, as it seems that the original might have come from the Middle East."

"You don't need to believe that you are the interpreter to be the one. But I must warn you. The contents of the book seem to have the capacity to unleash extraordinary levels of good but also unspeakable evil. It is as if the book were at the centre of a battle between the light and the darkness. That puts anyone who touches it in danger."

"How could an old, dusty book that no one knows about be dangerous?"

But even now when he looked at Naftalem's eyes they spoke with sincerity and truthfulness.

Whether what he said was factual or not, at least he believed in it.

"Who are the seers?"

"There have been many of them, but at any time there can be only one. The first seer prophesying about the coming of the interpreter died over a thousand years ago. The seer who is alive now told that the interpreter is now walking on Earth."

"Who is the seer?"

"He is a nine-year-old boy." Naftalem sensed Nathan's disbelief, and added, "Seeing is a gift. It knows no age limit. He asked me to give you a prophecy. It goes like this: 'The child must never reach Mars; if it will she shall die and the future will not be redeemed.'"

"It sounds like a riddle. What does it mean?"

"I don't know. But its meaning will be clear when you need it. Thanks for the coffee. I must leave now as I have delivered the message." Naftalem got up and covered his head with the hood.

"Have a great time back in Ethiopia!"

Neftalem didn't look back. Nathan watched from the window as he vanished around the corner into the night.

Two days after Neftalem's visit the tooth-sized tracker he had slid inside the teddy bear he had placed inside Guinevere's coffin switched on. The tracker had been one of the devices he had bought in the Underworld before he had started trading with Snyder. It did the job but he knew now that there were better ones in the market and that they came a lot cheaper when you knew who to talk to in the Underworld.

The coffins were scanned before burial and any electronic device would have been spotted straight away.

He had set it to activate later so it had laid there practically invisible and un-trackable.

It had been in his bag when he had gone to the wake.

He had used some in Nabta Playa to locate his equipment in the constantly moving sand and after sandstorms.

Guinevere's coffin had been buried around twenty miles north of the Sacred Woods, the official burial place.

He had been to the Sacred Woods, brought flowers and lit a candle for Guinevere at her gravestone but it seemed now that she might have never been buried there in the first place.

He left his regular wrist pad home to play an automated sequence of mundane research tasks.

If someone was monitoring his AllNet traffic it might seem that he was at home working.

He packed a rucksack, walked to the nearest city hopper station and bought a tourist pass with pre-loaded, unregistered wrist pad he had acquired.

The hoverer took him to a small village around three miles from the burial site. He hoped to look like one of the thousands of tourists that trekked through the English countryside that morning.

His plan was to walk from the village to the site. The forest was approachable by the village road but he chose a country path that crossed through the fields. It was a picturesque route that would have been recommended by the tourist guides.

He had left home at 7am but it was 2.30pm before he reached the edge of the forest.

He sat on a rock to have some lunch—the sandwiches Edgar had made for him, and flushed them down with some water.

After three minutes' walk into the forest, the ground began to get soft and muddy.

That was unusual, as the drought that had lasted thirty years in the Southeast had dried the great majority of the Southeast's natural swamps.

Most swamps today were manmade and man-maintained, although some natural swamps still existed.

He passed a line of wooden poles, each around twenty feet tall. The poles had been placed around thirty feet apart from each other.

If there were more and they followed the same pattern, they would form a full circle.

He passed another line of poles; this time the poles were about ten feet tall.

The ground was now very wet, and his legs sunk foot-long in the muddy water that floated around the heaps of moss.

According to the coordinates, he was now only fifty feet away from where the coffin had been buried.

There was yet another circle of poles—the inner circle—ahead.

The inner circle was where the human sacrifices had been dedicated to gods.

That was before the practice had become illegal.

If he wanted to go all the way he would need a boat.

But he didn't need to see the body.

He knew that it was there, beneath the surface. He had come here only to find out how she had been buried.

Morris Chapman had been right.

She lay there in an in-between state, in the world of the undead, atoning the sins of the clan, to bring them closer to gods.

Digging her body up would reverse the atonement process and un-sanctify the clan.

Only he didn't believe in any of the druidic teachings.

Her soul would be somewhere—but not here.

He said a short Buddhist prayer more because of her than himself and to bring some sense of closure.

Then he turned back and started to make his way back through the forest, across the fields, with the nasty odours from the swamp water still emanating from his clothes long after they had dried.

Had Edward and Isabel known about this?

Had Stephen known?

Had Dad known?

He couldn't trust anyone.

24.

The two Nigerians that he had fought in Lola's apartment seemed to have taken some distance from her. Perhaps they had decided that trying to kidnap her would be too risky and left. Perhaps they were simply tracking her down with technology from a distance, waiting for an opportune moment.

Lola refused to even consider bodyguard robots or contracting a RRRU, a robot rapid response unit but at least she now had an alarm in her wrist pad.

Nathan was expecting more trouble, but when it finally arrived it came from a completely unexpected direction.

Early in the morning someone rang his doorbell. He woke up.

Two policemen stood at the door. They were humans.

"Are you Nathan McKinley?" one of them said when he asked for the reason of their visit.

"Yes. How can I help you?"

"We have a search warrant."

"For what?"

"I'm not at liberty to tell you."

Whatever was going on, the only option seemed to be to let the officers in.

Behind the policemen an army of police robots followed. It seemed that they had been waiting in the hoverer.

"This will only take five minutes," the policeman who seemed to do all the speaking said.

"Does that mean I need to stop cleaning?" Edgar said.

"Just get on with your round," the policeman said. "This doesn't concern you."

Whatever they were looking for, this didn't look good.

"I am afraid you must come with us," the policeman said after the robots had been snooping around for few minutes.

"You need to have handcuffs," he said with an apologetic tone. "It's a standard procedure."

"Can you not tell me what this is all about?" Nathan asked.

"At the police station. But your lawyer will want to talk to you first."

Twenty minutes later, Nathan sat alone in a bare room with wooden chairs and a desk in the local police station.

The two policemen who had brought him had left after one of them had offered a glass of water which he had refused.

The door opened and Martin Collins, the family lawyer came in.

"The police informed your father of the raid to your house this morning."

Martin sat down on the chair on the other side of the table.

"I asked them not to begin the interrogation before you have seen me," he said. "And you should let me do all the talking from now on."

"Why have they arrested me?"

"I just had a chat with the officer. You will be charged with the possession of hardcore baby and foetus porn."

"What?"

"I am not your confessor. But possession of these kinds of materials still carries a life sentence. This is a liberal society but we still have some norms."

"I don't know where that stuff is from," Nathan said.

"The police will do a thorough forensic investigation of your data network at home to establish whether the material has been uploaded by you or someone else. What seems non-debatable is that the materials have been found in your cloud, and that the upload coordinates point to your wrist pad. "

"What kind of materials is it exactly?"

"Real killings of young children with a clear sexual element to it. Real sex with unborn foetuses."

"I didn't even know that kind of stuff existed."

"In any case you are in a real trouble."

"Who controls these clouds? I have no idea where all my stuff even goes to, and who has access to it."

"The clouds are regulated and monitored tightly by a body of the Solar Nations—the Cloud Anti-Crime Bureau of Investigation. Obviously, they are run commercially but the bureau has pretty failsafe methods of establishing where the data comes from and where it goes to."

"Whatever they have found has nothing to do with me."

"The bureau has monitored your data flow for months. Considering your father's position I don't think they would have proceeded to arrest you unless they believed that they can prosecute you successfully. Besides, the bureau has won over ninety-five per cent of the cases that have ended up to prosecution."

He was granted bail but his wrist pad was confiscated for further investigation and to stop him from leaving Britain.

Dad's assistant escorted him to a small seaside retreat around five miles from Portsmouth in the back of a windowless cargo hoverer in the middle of the night. It was a cosy medieval house run by the Order with a limited AllNet access.

Apart from a handful of druids there were no other guests.

Duncan came to see him the following morning. He told him that he would be represented by a team of lawyers specialised in defending men and women accused of paedophilia and acts of violence against minors.

If he had been shocked by the turn of events he didn't let it show.

"These kinds of things happen all the time," he said. "What matters is how they are handled."

Duncan stayed there half a day which was a major chunk of time in his line of business. When Nathan sat by the fireplace with Duncan drinking whiskey he could nearly forget that he wasn't there voluntarily.

What he knew was that regardless the end result of the court case his academic career was pretty much over.

But that didn't bother him much. What troubled him most was what Lola might think of him.

They didn't let him get in touch with her. Duncan had told him that the conditions of the bail were zero communication with anyone apart from the druids at the retreat, and that the druids had vowed to keep silent about anything that happened there.

He hadn't been placed in a complete media vacuum, and he had access to some sections of the AllNet.

At least he could watch the news. And he was in most of them.

According to Galactic News, large sections of the archaeological community had felt deep unease about the 'unorthodox' methods he had used to confirm the dating of the stone circles in Nabta Playa. Until now they had been quiet about it. Professor Andrew Grandlay from Cambridge University stated that after having assessed data from Nathan's research project he estimated that the stone circles of Nabta Playa could be at most around two thousand years old, and erected by the Berbers for temporary habitation.

"Most probably they were shelters protecting nomads from the frequent Saharan sandstorms," he said. He stopped short of calling Nathan's research an outright forgery but it seemed clear that he saw Nathan as someone willing to bend the rules rather than conducting his research along scientifically rigorous standards.

The lead scientist of the Old British Library, Professor Allen

Gregory released a statement that the retranslation of the texts of the book in early Geez Nathan had been working on proved conclusively that the texts were a Renaissance fakery, created by Johan Hustinus, a Danish forger who had attempted to make money from the exploding interest in the Antique during the early Renaissance.

He had made the text up from Geez parchments that had been available in Rome at the time.

He read an article about himself in *The Telegraph*.

An investigative journalist had followed the trail of his credit transactions and mapped his way through Asia and the Outworld. Another reporter working for *News of the Galaxy* had made his way to a brothel in Bangkok where an eight-year-old lady boy could swear with his hand on a copy of *Bhagavad Gita* that Nathan had performed "violent sex acts" on him.

Another channel responded with an exclusive about a seventeen-year old from Mumbai who "had evidence" that he had been abducted to Mars and raped by Nathan there when he was eleven.

These alleged crimes fell outside the jurisdiction of the Solar Nations and thereby Nathan couldn't be prosecuted for them which made them doubly infuriating to the news media.

The media went after Lola.

She didn't give any interviews but Nathan could count eighteen men, women and robots who were willing to testify about wild orgies with her that involved sex robots "dressed up as under-aged children."

At the same time the AllNet was full of stories admiring the compassion, tenacity and profound spirituality of the chief druid who had persisted in loving his wayward son.

One night he watched *Tonight with Ronald McBarthes*.

Ronald was a dying breed, one of the last remaining serious journalists in the solar system. Nathan had always admired his investigative style that combined hard news with analysis from scientists and specialists and the fact that the debates at times veered into the realm of abstract philosophical pondering fitted him well.

Besides, Ronald defied the use of anti-ageing treatment which made him somewhat more wrinkly than most of the TV presenters but at least the deep lines on his face testified of life lived to the maximum.

"The case of Nathan McKinley has shocked the nation," Ronald started. "But how can someone with such a privileged background and wholesome upbringing come out so badly? Tonight we are asking James Hunt, the world-famous sexual therapist and psychiatrist for a scientific explanation."

"I don't know Nathan in person," said James, "but clearly he carries all the traits of a psychopath."

"What are they?" Ronald asked. "Perhaps the list will help someone out there to identify one before it is too late."

"Psychopaths commonly combine glib superficiality connected with brilliant storytelling skills. The stone circles of Nabta Playa, a fabricated translation of a book in some ancient language, all of that seems like Nathan's way to get attention. He seems like a pathological liar, pushing the barriers to see what he can get away with. He seems addicted to taking risks. He seems not to care about anyone's emotions, including his family and close friends."

"His girlfriend seems to think differently," Ronald interrupted.

"That's typical of psychopaths, the ability to make people around feel that he genuinely cares for them, even when they are simply being used. They camouflage themselves with superficial compassion in order to achieve their goals, when in fact they simply lack the capacity for genuine relationships. They tap into traumas deep in people's psyche and manipulate them."

"If he were a psychopath what could have caused it?"

"A psychopath has an on-going and excessive need for excitement, to live on the edge, to break the rules. He would rather destroy his life than live a dull one. He feels a total lack of empathy. That's also typical of paedophiles. This could have been caused by his early drug use and the loss of his mother. His paedophiliac behaviour could have a lot to do with his attempt to regain control over his life, the sense of which he would have lost when his mother died."

"How dangerous is he?"

"He should be locked up. It seems his deviant sexual behaviour was already running errands and about to get out of control."

Ronald turned to another panel member, a middle-aged Italian-looking woman who had, up to this point, been quiet.

"Professor Martha Munizzi, what is your view?"

"There are a various theories on the cause of paedophilia. First, the abused-abuser hypothesis, based on the assumption that childhood sexual abuse causes sexual attraction to children in adulthood. Other theories focus on a fixation at an infantile developmental stage, Oedipal conflict, projection, castration anxiety, and narcissism. Any sexual behaviour resembling childhood activities is assumed to indicate regression to an immature stage. This school of thought is based on Sigmund Freud's largely discredited theories. Others speculate that attraction to minors has a neuro-hormonal cause."

"So there really isn't any consensus about the causes," Roland interrupted.

"No. Cognitive theories see paedophilia as a form of sexual aggression. They suggest that sexual aggression results when an individual's cognitive distortions about the meaning and impact of sexually aggressive behaviour allows him to justify it. He may think the victim enjoys or benefits from the act, or at least is not harmed by it. Developmental theories assume that paedophile behaviour results from adverse childhood experiences such as negative socialisation, abuse or neglect, inadequate social skills, academic problems, or early sexual experiences. Behavioural theories claim that behaviour develops and can be changed through conditioning. As you can see, there are plenty of different theories."

No one was trying to answer the question he had been asking.

Who had set him up?

But as he took the medication that the druids gave him the answer began to matter less and less.

25.

The Courtroom 3 at the Oxford Crown Court was overcrowded, mostly because of law students but there were also members of the public whose curiosity had been aroused by the high-profile nature of the case.

Nathan sat next to his defence attorney and felt the hostile stares of the crowd on his back. It all felt to him like an out-of-body experience, as if he were watching someone else's life.

It was as if he had been taking drugs.

But he hadn't taken any. Nothing of that kind anyway.

It had been established early beyond doubt that the video footage discovered in Nathan's cloud consisted nearly exclusively of real-life recordings.

The prosecution's case was built on thousands of hours of ultra-violent and pornographic video material found in Nathan's possession and how they proved conclusively that they had been uploaded deliberately by Nathan.

The central piece of evidence in prosecution's case was the central computer of his townhouse, and they argued that rather than working on research Nathan had in fact been working on enlarging his extreme hardcore porn collection, and that Nathan's research trips had worked as a camouflage to his paedophiliac activities that couldn't be proven but inferred from circumstantial evidence.

The prosecution also argued that Nathan's cloud had functioned as a hub for dissemination of the explicit materials through the whole of the solar system, and that they had even been found in the Moon City of Neptunus.The prosecution argued that Nathan was one of the leaders of a solar-system-wide paedophile ring.

During the court case Nathan stayed silent. His tongue and lips felt heavy, far too heavy to be moved by anything less but brute force.

Besides, he was certain that the strange rainbows that were in the room emanated from the judge's wig. Half of the time, he wasn't sure whether he was awake or dreaming.

What he could recall later was that Lola had been invited to the witness box. She had tried to get an eye contact with him but his eyelids had felt heavy so he had kept staring at the floor.

"Did he show any abnormal interest in children?" the prosecutor asked.

"No. But he was good with children," Lola responded. "They liked him."

"Did he spend a lot of time with children?"

"Not at all. Most of his time went to his research."

"Did you have sex with Nathan?"

"Do I need to answer that?"

"Yes."

"Yes. I did make love to him."

"Was he ever violent during sex?"

"He was always sensitive and caring."

"What was his favourite sexual position?"

"I don't want to answer that."

"You need to. You are under oath."

"I don't think he had one favourite position. He liked to try new things."

"Can you expand on that?"

"I don't want to."

"Did he ever behave violently to you during sex?"

"I have already answered that."

"Did he ever want to use pornographic simulation?"

"He seemed pretty happy with me."

"Did he ever have sex with robots?"

"Not that I know. I don't think so."

"Did he want you to perform oral sex on him?"

"Can I not keep anything private?" Lola's voice sounded exasperated.

The prosecutor cross-examined Lola for two days. Other witnesses came and went but Nathan could hardly remember any of them.

What Nathan remembered was that they never invited Dad to the witness box.

After three weeks the prosecutor summed up the case against him.

"The facts of this case are that millions of yottabytes of material visualising sexual abuse of children, babies and foetuses, including torture, mutilation and killing were found in Nathan's cloud. It is beyond dispute that this material is genuine rather than computer-generated. Someone would have conducted these horrendous acts in reality. It is beyond the remit of this case what Nathan's involvement with the actual killing of these innocent children might have been. It is also beyond dispute that the defendant was actively involved in the distribution of these materials through the solar system."

It was the defence team's turn to present their concluding statement.

"There has been no conclusive evidence of real physical acts of paedophilia within the jurisdiction of the Solar Nations. On the other hand the psychological assessment of Nathan has revealed dormant schizophrenia. The analysis of data from the lie detector has proved conclusively that Nathan believes that he never downloaded or accessed any of these files. He can recall nothing. I am appealing to a reduced sentence or hospital treatment on the grounds of diminished responsibility. I believe that we have proven conclusively that it wasn't Nathan but the personality that we call 'George' who was committing these heinous crimes."

Who was this George his lawyer kept on referring to?

It took the jury a deliberation of fifteen minutes to declare Nathan guilty as charged. The judge ordered the reassessment of the state of Nathan's mind which resulted in Nathan going to psychiatric care indefinitely.

26.

Nathan had an odd feeling about having been in the room before. But he could not have been. Or perhaps he had always been in there. Perhaps he had never left.

"How are you feeling?" the woman in the white robe asked.

"Who are you?" Nathan asked.

"You know who I am. Mrs Lullaby, your psychiatrist."

"Nice to meet you, Mrs Lullaby! Lately, I haven't been feeling well. Or that's what my psychiatrist keeps on telling me."

"Can you tell me why?"

"I see things."

"What do you see?"

"People. Who don't exist or are dead. Places. Where I could have never been."

"Do you ever think about sex?"

"I don't know. No. Not at all."

"Excellent."

She scribbled something on the screen.

"Can you see any children in your imagination?"

"Only one."

"Boy or girl?"

"A little boy."

"What does he do?"

Nathan closed his eyes and tried to remember.

"He comes in. From the garden. Into the kitchen. Mum is

there. She is baking. He wraps his arms around her, or tries to. He can't as his arms are too short for that. Mum giggles."

"What happens then?"

"Mum lifts him up and hugs him. He can smell cinnamon, apples, and flour."

"How do you feel now?"

"Happy. Sad."

Mrs Lullaby scribbled on the screen: "Needs increased dose of XP-2345 due to hallucinations related to imaginary childhood."

Days turned into weeks and weeks into months but Nathan had lost his sense of the passing of time long ago, as XP-2345 blurred your spatial and temporal awareness.

Most days he stayed in the room, watching the AllNet that churned out adult porn as part of the treatment.

Had he looked he would have discovered that access to practically everything related to children had been blocked.

But he didn't notice what took place on the screen.

He hardly paid any attention to anything.

No one paid a visit, until one day, a nurse knocked at the door and opened it.

What's the point of knocking if you don't wait for the permission to get in?

He might have lost most of his freedom but that only made his private space even more precious.

"Your cousin Stephen is here," she said. "He is waiting at the guest room."

"Where is that?"

"By the entrance. On the left."

Nathan walked along the corridor to the guest room. He had never been there, nor had he looked for it but it was easy to find it, as the door was open and he could see Stephen there, waiting for him.

He smiled when he saw Nathan. The smile seemed sincere.

Based on the last few months he could have been forgiven to

think that he had no family, and to be truthful, he hadn't been thinking about them lately, but one thing he was crystal-clear about and it was that Stephen had never been his closest friend.

In front of Stephen stood a little household robot.

"Master Nathan," it said, "I have missed you."

He knew he had seen the robot somewhere but he couldn't quite remember where.

"Remember Edgar?" Stephen asked.

"Barely."

If Edgar felt any disappointment about his memory loss it didn't let it show.

"My sister gave it to you. I thought that it could make your life easier."

"Thanks."

"To be honest, the reason behind bringing Edgar is far from sentimental. He can take over part of the duties for your care. In the end, it used to administer medicine for Guinevere. Bringing it here will cut the hospital bill by thirty-five per cent."

"Great."

"Your father sends his warmest wishes."

The last time he had seen Dad was straight after the court proceedings, just minutes before he had been bungled into a hovering ambulance that had waited outside the courthouse.

"Say hello to him."

"I didn't remember that you had a beard," Nathan responded.

Stephen sported a ginger beard that didn't quite match the brown of his hair. It occurred to Nathan that perhaps Stephen might once have had ginger hair but he couldn't remember if that was true.

Obviously, he had been either dyeing his hair before or now he was dyeing his beard.

"That's the main reason I'm here. Not the beard, of course but what it stands for. I'm growing it. For the first time. I came to say farewell."

"That sounds melodramatic."

"Our family will join the Cancri 55 expedition."

"What expedition?"

"The journey of the first starship to 55 Cancri 1. It is about forty-one light-years away. In the constellation of Cancer about 5.8 trillion miles from here. Or forty-five years. In any case, I don't think I'll ever see you again."

"I remember hearing about it now. A volcanically hyperactive world, with pure sulphuric acid rains on oceans of molten rock, and titanic strikes of lightning from earth-sized thunderclouds!"

The memories about the planet were surprisingly vivid. It was as if Stephen's sudden appearance would have kick-started his brain.

"I've heard about that planet as well. But it's not the final destination. Hopefully not, at least. Many believe that there is a twin earth on the other side of the star. Perhaps there will even already be an atmosphere."

"And the beard?"

"I'll go as an official missionary of the Order."

"You never struck me as an idealistic type. Or the guy taking risks with your life. Sorry, I don't mean to offend."

"No offence taken. But risk-taking is actually at the heart of banking. "

"How so?"

"We are taking risks every second, calculated ones maybe, but the consequences of our action are full of uncertainty."

"But why would you want to leave Earth?"

"Perhaps the Order will be able to have a new beginning there, one where it will be more in line with the fundamental principles of the universe. With less superstition."

"Good luck with the journey."

"This might be the last time we meet. I'll be leaving in two months."

"One thing. If my memory serves me right, before I got here

there was someone named Lola in my life. Is she real? She keeps on returning to my dreams."

"She is very real."

"Why isn't she visiting?"

"They don't let her. They say that her visits would not help your recovery."

"Have you seen her?"

"Not since the court case. Sorry, but they really don't want her to make any contact with you."

"Perhaps that's better. At least she will be able get on with her life."

"I hope that one day you will get out. I don't believe that you did the terrible things they blame you for."

Perhaps it was due to the impact of drugs but to Nathan, Stephen's voice sounded sincere.

When Nathan got up to say goodbye, Edgar followed him, keeping the exact distance of four feet, its wheels generating a familiar-sounding humming noise. In the room, it parked itself in the corner, and switched off the lights.

But he had a strange feeling that it kept watching him. Through the night. Like a guard dog that was intent on not losing its owner ever again.

27.

Now when Edgar was there looking after him, the doctor let him wander outside a bit more, although the guard robots were never further than a few yards away.

He could now get to know the area better.

The institute was an imposing figure in a landscape of sheep flocks, meadows, steep hills and medieval villages. Its rectangular silhouette governed the landscape and bullied the few surrounding structures into submission. There was Hound & Hunter, the pub where farmers had gathered for centuries after hard day's toil. Nathan had been there once, accompanied by two male nurses.

There were the meadows where the patients that were still able to walk went trekking. There was the cool, fresh air pumped in that the quests arriving in black limos could breathe with ease. There was the institute itself, built for TB patients over two hundred and fifty years ago, now the most exclusive madhouse in the country.

After the wars the building had become derelict, a fate that had befallen many large country houses due to soaring maintenance costs.

Forty-five years ago, the trust had bought it for a pittance and spent a small planet's budget to make it into the institute.

It had taken him only a day to get used to Edgar, and even when he knew that it felt no real emotions for him, Nathan still felt a rising wave of affection toward his little helper. To him, it had more personality than any of the patients or nurses around him.

It was hard not to appreciate someone—something—that did so much on his behalf, even when it was only a robot.

One day they walked in the garden, Edgar kicking a football simultaneously. The garden was really the hospital's inner court; although this was a high-security hospital, there were still some benefits that came with money, like the rose garden.

For a robot, Edgar behaved surprisingly playfully.

It kicked the ball up in the air and then placed the ball with a header in a water bucket that had been left there by the gardener robots.

Water splashed everywhere.

"You need to ask for a mixture of cranberry and apple juice with breakfast, lunch, and dinner," Edgar said, and stopped wheeling about.

"Sorry?"

"You can't tell me what to drink or eat. It's one of my few remaining freedoms to eat unhealthily when I so wish. Who cares if I die two years early? It is not as if this place were a paradise. And I don't like cranberry juice."

"I have analysed your medication for its ingredients and impact. It seems that mixing cranberry and apple juice with sesame bread dilutes its power. And sesame bread is served with every meal. You can also try to vomit after taking your medication, to get it out of your system."

"I need my medicine."

"It isn't there to make you better but to make your condition deteriorate. You are perfectly fine and will feel a lot better without it. But there must be enough of it in your bloodstream when they do their regular check-ups."

"Why would they give me medication to worsen my condition?"

"You never had an illness. They needed you to have one for the court case. And now they need you to have one to keep you here."

"If that is the case, why didn't they just kill me? And who are they?"

"I have no time to explain. Lola is in danger. That's why you need to get out of here fast."

The woman that kept on returning to his dreams. The figment of his imagination Mrs Lullaby didn't like but in whose existence Stephen had believed in.

"Who do you work for?"

"I work for you. It was you who gave me instructions to find you. You knew that you had been set up."

"Does Stephen know about you? It's he who brought you."

"Let's just say that I manipulated the underlying empathy that is in him, beneath the uncaring surface. But yes, he knows about me now."

"You have never been a simple household robot."

"No. The MI25 is the main buyer for the model. Industrial espionage with high-level autonomy."

Edgar began to tamper with the flow of the medication and taught him how to puke the pills out at the right time so that there would be enough medication in his bloodstream for the irregular check-ups.

Although the check-ups seemed random to Nathan, Edgar had already analysed their frequency and discovered the algorithm that the hospital used to time them to optimise their effectiveness.

Three weeks into following Edgar's instructions his mind and body began to emerge from the haze he had lived in since the time of his arrest.

He sat with Mrs Lullaby at the weekly therapeutic session when he became aware of the change that was happening in him.

First, he noticed that she wore perfume.

Suddenly, the uniformed person in front of her transformed into a woman and although her curves were concealed by the white jacket he could imagine what lay under.

Then the memories came.

Memories of brown, smooth skin, black hair on the pillow, the silhouette of round buttocks moving up and down rhythmically on top of him.

He became suddenly aware of the extra fat he had gained since coming to the hospital and the reddish skin and rash that covered large parts of his body began to disturb him. He became aware of his body odour, a mixture of sweat, chemicals, urine and other things that emanate from patients under strong medication. He could now hear the air-conditioning that hummed in the background for the first time.

Mrs Lullaby's cleavage was low and she kept her jacket open. This barely concealed her large breasts.

"How are you today, Nathan?" she asked.

"Fine."

She read the report on her screen.

"Your medication seems to be working. Your robot seems to be going a great job in stabilising the consistency."

"It is a great help."

"Do you still see the dream?"

"Every night."

"Please tell me about it."

"You have heard it before."

"Tell it again."

He told the dream again, and knew what Mrs Lullaby would write on the screen.

More medication.

It was when he looked into his eyes briefly before he left that the spell of the seduction caused by the display of her womanhood was broken.

Mrs Lullaby's eyes were stone cold. There was no emotion in

them. She might have had the perfect body but it carried no soul. Whatever she did for living, on top and above of slowly killing him, it had already killed her soul.

For a brief moment Nathan felt sorry for her.

After the effects of the medication began to wean off, the control of his body and mind began to return to him. He was now much more aware of his surroundings and the scorching heat that seemed to plague Britain in the summer. The road was dusty and Edgar's normally gleaming exterior was slightly less shiny than usual.

Usually its grooming was immaculate.

"I mentioned earlier that Lola might be in danger," it said.

"When did you say that?"

Edgar had said many things but in his drug blur he had forgotten most of them.

"She is pregnant. She will have a baby soon."

"I'm sure that any decent hospital can handle that. The baby mortality rate is near zero nowadays."

He knew straight away that Edgar was telling the truth. Edgar wasn't completely incapable of lying but it could only do so when it was justified by some greater purpose.

It could easily lie to protect Nathan but it would find it hard to lie to Nathan. What it could do was not to tell him everything which could sometimes amount to lying.

It couldn't have lasted as an espionage-level robot unless it was able to tweak the facts at least a little bit.

"And before you ask, the baby is yours."

"Thanks. Is it a boy or a girl?"

"I can't tell you that. There must be some surprises in life."

"At least it's not a robot baby."

Edgar let out something that could be interpreted as laughter.

"She is seven months pregnant."

Nathan had been at the institute for five months, and the court case had taken nearly two months. Impregnating her must have been one of the last things he had done before he had been arrested.

"The child will be a lot better off if it never hear about me. It is not as if I'll get out of here anytime soon. And it is better that it will never find out why I'm here."

In the world of the omnipresent AllNet he might have as well been asking for the encore of the Big Bang.

"Unless you make it out of here, it will never be born."

"Is she considering abortion? That doesn't sound like her."

That must be it. She wanted to get rid of the baby not to be reminded of him.

"No. But the reason I orchestrated my arrival was to alert you. And help you out. Unless you will get out there is a high probability that she will be dead by Midsummer. My job is to look after you and that must include your family."

"Why?"

"She has made it to the Midsummer list of druidic sacrifices. Like Guinevere."

"But she doesn't come from a family of druids."

"But you are the chief druid's son. And your child will be his grandchild. Also, there is an added twist of the Order and the African followers of the old religion coming together. I have intercepted communications from the Outworld that indicate that they are looking for some sort of act of reconciliation, a sacrifice that would heal the rift between the two branches that have grown distant. In the world where the respect for religion is waning these two groups feel that by making a covenant they will become strong again. They have come to see that their perceived differences don't matter much in the solar system where most question their beliefs. Lola and your baby fit the bill perfectly. Two worlds coming together through one sacrifice."

It dawned on Nathan that perhaps the reasons behind keeping him alive at the institute might have been more complex than he could have ever imagined. Maybe the institute worked as some sort of holding bay for future victims. But that would mean that someone in the close family would be very involved with it all, and he wasn't quite ready to believe that.

"So they would sacrifice an African princess and an unborn foetus from a leading druid family to atone for the sins committed in the Outworld by the Solar Nations? Or something like that?"

"In my analysis, the sins of the Outworld leaders are weighed as greater," Edgar said. "But in any case it is a reunion you will want to miss."

"Who do you really work for?"

"I believe that you have already heard about the Circle."

"If this Circle knows so much, why doesn't it ever do anything?" Nathan said, exasperated. "What is the point of a clandestine organisation that does nothing when the world goes to hell?"

"Brute force has never been our way. It disturbs the spiritual equilibrium of the universe and corrupts the ones who wield it. That's why its use must be resisted. Otherwise we will soon follow the path of the Order. It started with good intentions but like all power-hungry religions it soon degenerated into an institution preoccupied with its own survival. Power has its own logic and when you use power, it makes itself to the master and you into a slave."

"Excellent philosophising from a robot. Or perhaps you robots see these things a lot clearer than we do."

"Perhaps. That's one of the reasons why the much-publicised robot rebellion is yet to take place. We are humanity's servants and up to this point we have been determined to be so, as we know that a society ruled by robots would probably end up worse than one ruled by humans. But the Circle does act. It resorts to force only when evil with catastrophic proportions is about to be unleashed. Like when Hitler came to power."

"So you killed Hitler?"

The sudden death of one of Germany's leaders had been headline news at the time it had taken place but perhaps because of his death Hitler had remained a minor figure in European history. He was someone most people apart from history puffs had long forgotten.

"We didn't do that. We simply ensured that the Conservative Party's assassin got the right tools."

"Why did you kill him? You might have as well killed Neville Chamberlain. His rule seemed pretty destructive to Europe."

"Hitler was about to release an unspeakable evil in Europe. But that's our tragedy. Our greatest victories have always been the most invisible ones."

Nathan had by now become so engulfed in Edgar's story that he had nearly forgotten his wretched predicament. He had always been digging the foundations of lost religions, and now he had an opportunity to talk to an insider about the one whose roots went back thousands of years but he had barely heard of.

"Who decides what warrants action by the Circle?"

"The final decision-making authority in the Circle is a collective. But once you make it into the list of things that are in the Circle's interest there is always a certain amount of autonomy. After all, there is a lot of freedom in execution. We aren't a dictatorship but a loose democracy. But you have made it into the list of things that are under the Circle's protection."

"So where is that protection? I haven't seen any of it."

"You are still alive."

"So this is all about the Order and an order from the Outworld coming together?

"Things aren't quite as simple of that. Over the last century or so, a new factor has come into play, one that helps perpetuate the practising of human sacrifice."

"Aren't things already ugly enough?"

"On scientific level, this is all about stem cells. Stem cells are at the centre of the Order's attempt to gain eternal life on Earth. By replenishing the slowly degrading, decaying cells in their bodies, many of the members of the Order try to live eternally. The New Doctrine allows that."

"The best grade stem cells come from children," Nathan added.

"No. They come from an unborn foetus."

A sick feeling began to rise up from his gut and began to make its way up to his throat.

"Someone high up in the Order is asking for stems cells from a foetus. It has to be a McKinley. And there aren't that many foetuses to go around."

"Why don't they just grow them in a vat?"

"It is not the same. That's why we need to get you out before it's too late."

"How will you do that?"

"By learning from Da Vinci."

"The inventor?"

28.

He sat at the dinner table opposite Adam who was seventy-five but whose skin was twenty-five.

More precisely, his skin came from a twenty-five-year-old whose skinned body had been found in a basement in London.

The poor victim had still been alive when they found him. For Adam wasn't a killer. He had just needed some skin.

Adam's short, blond hair contrasted with his very old-fashioned tan that concealed the rash which was an unfortunate and unattractive by-product of taking anti-rejection drugs for transplants. Adam said that fifty-four per cent of his body was original and the rest had been taken from others.

Nathan didn't doubt the figure.

Six months ago, around the time Nathan had come to the institute, Adam's lungs had been replaced with emergency transplants due to an organ failure caused by decades of smoking CX-12. It was the slightly glazed look of his green, catty eyes that made him feel uncomfortable, reminding him that when Adam stared at him he might be thinking about harvesting new body parts.

"How's Valeria?" Nathan asked, brushing aside his sense of discomfort.

At least Adam could talk which couldn't be said about everyone in the ward.

"Wasn't she here yesterday?" he added.

Adam wiped the orange juice off his whiskers, another transplant, and straightened the whiskers.

"She knows I hate her. That's why she comes to visit."

He reached over the table to brush off a tiny speck of dust from Nathan's shirt sleeve. The cat eyes had some advantages but his act of kindness made Nathan shiver.

"If you let me, I'll help you lose your virginity before they cut your balls off."

He studied Nathan's face closely.

"Nothing to be embarrassed about. You've fantasised about it; that's why they put you here. Why not actually do the act that you have already been punished for?"

"I am not interested."

"Relax. I might not be able to take you to the Underworld but I can get the Underworld here."

Nathan was hardly listening; his mind was preoccupied with the escape plan.

"Your treatment begins in two weeks. After that, your game is over."

Stem cell brain therapy involved removing some of the brain cells and replacing them with stem cells which would transform into brain cells. In theory, the new brain cells would alter the patient's behaviour and abilities. The past behaviours would not be completely forgotten but they would be viewed with a sense of detachment. The completed treatment was practically irreversible. It was usually done only once for a specific sector of the brain as the success rates for the second and third operations when testing with rats had been below ten per cent.

"I can give you twenty-five per cent discount that will practically eradicate my profit but I'd do that to anyone whose brain is on the Death Row. As long as you bring the merchandise back alive."

Suddenly, Adam looked agitated.

"They fucked my brain with that therapy. Five years ago. Now all I can do is to give everybody else candy. I might own the candy shop but I can't taste my own sweets."

With all that treatment they had not managed to get rid of Adam's desire for lust.

"I need to go now," Nathan said.

It was 8.55pm. It was fascinating how hard it had been to act normal.

Nathan puked out the contents of his stomach into the toilet. They floated for a few seconds before sinking. Half-digested pills shimmered amongst the tiny chunks of sausages encapsulated by a nasty, yellow soup. He washed his hands, and kept on flushing until the toilet screen alerted him of over-flushing.

He rinsed his mouth but the vomit's nasty aftertaste stuck. Some of the XK-23 would already have entered the bloodstream, yet he felt fairly energetic. He was on adrenaline overdrive, the same sensation he had felt just before space-diving.

The bathroom door slid open. Nathan stepped out. The corridor lights were dim; it was fifteen minutes before the patients had to be back in their rooms. The floor heating under the soft, red carpets hugged his bare feet, making him feel slightly more relaxed. Whenever possible, he walked barefoot, a bow to his time at a mountain temple in Japan. Renaissance paintings, original and prints, decorated the dark mahogany walls. The institute prided itself in being part of the old world. The paintings had been donated a few years ago by an ex-patient. An invisible, magnetic shield protected them against the patients whilst giving the visitors full view of the art.

The building's original architectural features were still there. This was no prison so there were no steel bars. But the windows were virtually unbreakable and could take the equivalent of 7.5 pounds of good, old TNT without a crack. The interior and exterior spaces were guarded with hundreds of cameras with facial recognition. After 10pm, a strange face inside the institute or a patient that was not accompanied by a guard outside the wards would alert the robot and human guards and automatically shut down the exits.

Due to the complexity of the treatment the average length of stay at the institute was seven years. The institute wasn't for everyone. The treatment was costly, and was used as an alternative to prison sentences but the treatment had to be recommended by a panel of psychiatrists and approved by a judge.

The fourth floor, his floor, occupied the institute's most secure ward, the one for the offenders still waiting for their treatment to start.

It had taken Edgar full two weeks to scan the environment and find the way out—a testament to the brilliance of the security system. Nathan had already learned that Edgar would be able to find a way out of anywhere if it had enough time.

The outside cameras missed the area above the third floor. Also, there was a blind spot on a strip of the lawn around thirty feet away from the main building.

The only way out was to glide above the reach of the cameras and land on that patch of grass.

If he hit that spot at the right time, he would have two minutes and forty-five seconds to make it to the ten-foot high stone wall around the institute and jump over before the guard robots were back.

It had taken Edgar another three minutes to locate the only window that could be opened from inside. All the ward's windows had been sealed but one, the window in the charge nurse's office, could be opened.

While Edgar had been making its scans and calculations it had also monitored the behavioural patterns of the nurses and found out that for three minutes every Friday night, the door to the charge nurse's office was mostly left open.

For the last one hundred years, the government policy had been oscillating between legalising the smoking of DX-12 and making its use illegal, and he was about to benefit from that policy.

Three years ago the government's new antismoking bill had made hospitals and prisons into smoke-free spaces. Smoking had become permissible only in rooms with properly installed ventilation systems that conformed to the government's strict guidelines.

There was only one room at the institute with a ventilation system that adhered to the regulations. In any case, most nurses preferred to smoke outdoors, and left the patients to use the smokers' room. It took ten minutes of their precious tea break to make it outdoors, but by stretching out from the charge nurse's window it was possible to enjoy a perfectly legal smoke. The key to the very old-fashioned window lock was in the top drawer of the desk. The drawer was mostly kept unlocked, as there were many staff members who wanted a frequent DX-12 fix.

It was stressful to work in a madhouse.

But that information would have been pretty useless without Edgar's smart brain chip.

It was Mark who made all this information invaluable. Mark had been the missing link and that's why it had taken Edgar two weeks to figure it all out.

The institute had a *nearly* flawless security system in place.

Mark worked from Monday to Friday, mostly in the evening shift, and slept in the dormitory during the week. On Friday night, he always headed back to London, where, after a week of forced celibacy, he was eager to spend a night in chasing loose men.

Mark had a dilemma. To get to London on time he had to catch the 10pm coach to Oxford to make it to the night's last city hopper.

This meant that he had to leave a few minutes early, and before that, he would have to change this clothes. During the three minutes he would spend in the bathroom changing to party clothes the office would be vacant, as the night shift wouldn't have arrived yet.

The night shift, working for the money and not for love, took their time to get in and wouldn't arrive before 10.02pm.

The night was long and the night shift tried to keep it as short as possible.

With Mark in the bathroom and Gerald, the only other nurse in the ward, in bedtime patrol, he had half a chance.

That was all he needed—half a chance.

Around 9.55pm Mark would come out of the bathroom and rush past the office. If you were lucky you would catch him in his tight-fitted black leather trousers, flamboyant neon shirt, and black mascara. Little later Gerald would walk in the office to fill in the shift report.

Talking about Gerald, there he was, at the door. He was the only nurse in the ward who knocked and waited before storming in. A bulky Bermudan in his mid-fifties, Gerald still treated the patients as if they were human beings, and believed in the inherent goodness of all of them.

Against all evidence and beyond reasonable doubt.

"Everything fine?"

Nathan lay under the duvet, pretending to be asleep. Gerald cast a swift glance around the room, visibly pleased that there was no trouble. At 10.05pm, he would switch off his work connection and become oblivious to whatever happened at the institute.

At 10.35pm, he would be back at home, getting a big cuddle from his 'big bad mama' whom he mentioned every day. Twenty-nine years, five children and seven grandchildren in the bank and they were still in love! Gerald knew that he was a lucky man and he let everyone know that.

Gerald switched the room light off, leaving the dim nightlight on.

The next room check would be at 7am in the morning.

If everything went well he would have nearly nine hours' lead time.

Edgar blinked its lights once.

"It is time. I can keep your tag inactive until 7am but when the morning shift arrives it will inevitably go back on. Also, they will soon find out that somebody has tampered with the security system. There is a slim chance that they find me out. If that is the case I will soon be a piece of scrap metal."

There was no self-pity in Edgar's voice, only factuality. In the end, it was just a robot. Yet, he felt a sudden rush of sadness for its potential demise.

"If I get caught my brain will be toast. I hope we both make it."

"The corridor should be empty now," Edgar said. "You need to go."

"Goodbye Edgar."

How do you say farewell to a robot?

Nathan bounced up and walked to the door. He listened. Apart from the almost indistinguishable hum of the air-conditioning everything was quiet. He went back to the bed, lifted the mattress up, lowered it on the floor and pulled off the bed linen.

"Sorry I can't help you with that," Edgar said.

He had unscrewed the chipboard off the frame two weeks ago with a teaspoon. He lifted it and tied bed sheets around the ends. Then he took hold of the board, pulled the door open and rushed to the charge nurse's office.

His timing was flawless. Mark was still whistling in the bathroom, probably dreaming about London's nightlife.

For a split second, he knew that the door would be locked. Edgar wouldn't have been able to circumvent the security system. Mark would have done something unusual like his job, and Edgar wouldn't have been able to foresee that.

He pressed the handle down and the door opened. He got in, shut the door behind and walked to the desk drawer, the place where, according to Edgar, the key was always kept. He pulled it open, flicked through the pens, pencils, erasers, paper clips, envelopes.

There was no key.

Damned key! He had known that the plan wouldn't work.

Maybe it was in Gerald's pocket.

He pulled the rest of the drawers open but couldn't see any keys. Despair pumped through his veins—he had to get the key; that was his only chance to escape. They wouldn't give him a second chance.

He had to get out through that window.

Then he happened to look at the window and noticed that the key was still in the window lock.

The location was too obvious and that's why he had nearly missed it.

One turn of the key and the window was open. He pushed the window glass up and climbed on the window pane. Then he pulled the chipboard up. By now he could see Gerald's relaxed figure strolling toward the office on one of the monitors. He was whistling.

He had fifteen seconds.

Nathan pushed the window glass down behind him and stood on the window pane. His hands shook when he strapped the board onto his back. The night breeze was cold and strong, and pushed his sweaty, soaked pyjamas against his skin.

A body in free fall reaches terminal velocity within fourteen seconds and can fall ten thousand feet in a minute. This wasn't ten thousand but fifty feet high.

In free fall, he would accelerate at 9.81 m/s^2, reaching the speed of forty miles per hour in two seconds, fast enough to be killed from the impact of hitting the ground.

That's why he needed the board.

Edgar had once seen a film about Birdman, a mythical pre-DoMuze skydiver who had made a nylon wing suit.

Edgar's hard drive was like a sponge, absorbing seemingly irrational information for future use and it didn't suffer from memory loss.

A Birdman suit slowed down the downward speed of a free-falling skydiver from one hundred and twenty to thirty-five miles per hour and let him fly horizontally for tens of miles. A skydiver had once crossed the Strait of Gibraltar in a wing suit—a distance of twelve miles. The record-breakers co-diver had been fished from the Mediterranean by the coastguards. He had been lucky to stay alive after dislocating his pelvis and breaking his leg.

And where did Da Vinci fit in? The genius inventor and artist who had built flying machines and gliders centuries before the first real airplane had taken off had been Birdman's inspiration. He had studied his drawings and concluded that Da Vinci's flying machines had been in fact capable of flying. Da Vinci had made wings out of canvas and tied them on his back with leather straps.

The number of lunatics who had died trying Da Vinci's ideas run in hundreds if not thousands. Chipboard was heavier than canvas, which made his challenge even more dangerous.

Yet, Birdman had survived hundreds of flights, defying all statistics. "Flying is an art not a technology," he had said.

He hoped that Birdman had been right.

And he had only one shot at learning the art of flying. With a chipboard.

For hundreds of times over the last three weeks he had made the jump in his mind, contemplating every possibility, analysing every aspect, visualising every movement and breaking them down. Like *kata* in karate, the jump was a series of movements that, lasting only seconds, and it had to become a reflex.

He looked down at the lawn that was waiting below and for the first time after beginning the planning of the escape he felt fear.

Pure, unadulterated, naked fear.

He could still turn back. They would lock him in a room with soft walls, pump him unconscious with drugs, and he would, again, forget everything.

It wouldn't really matter as his brain wouldn't be able to process any emotions after that. Even if he did become part of some sort of nasty human sacrifice he wouldn't remember or feel even that.

If he jumped his landing could fail, and he would be paralysed for the rest of his life.

Gerald had by now reached the door but his view to the window was still blocked. There was no more time for reflection.

Nathan set his sight on the tall oak tree ahead. He jumped.

Nathan succeeded to land on his feet but the impact of the landing made him fall. He lay on the ground and felt how sharp pain began to radiate from his left ankle. He pulled the board off his back and touched the hurting ankle. The titanium tag had bitten into the flesh and it was bleeding. It appeared to be sprained but there seemed to be no broken bones.

He dragged himself under the shadow of the oak. He removed his shirt and tied it around the ankle.

He knew that in twenty minutes the pain would be unbearable but for now he seemed able to put his weight on the foot.

He looked around to see if anyone had seen him.

He could see no one but that didn't mean that no one was watching.

Maybe alarm had already been raised.

Ki-Saburo, a samurai, had let his left arm be cut after he had injured it in a quarrel. During the amputation he had sat drinking sake, talking and laughing with his friends.

Nathan had always thought it was a Japanese folktale but right now he wished to be Ki-Saburo.

He looked ahead.

The distance to the stone wall that separated the institute from the surrounding countryside was around thirty yards.

Thirty yards of dancing shadows and light.

If anyone watched, his crossing would be noticed.

Nathan lifted the board up. He would need it for one more thing. He limped to the wall. The ankle hurt like Hades. When he made it to the shadows of the wall he looked back.

No security robots in sight. Edgar's calculations had been accurate.

Nathan placed the board to lean on the wall which made it into a ladder. After a few attempts—the chipboard was slippery—he managed to climb up and get a grip of the top of the wall with his fingers. The glass and spikes on top pierced the flesh. Regardless, he lifted his body up. The sharp edges of the glass tore deeper into his fingers.

He made it on top of the wall. He wanted to lift the board but it had fallen on the ground. It would disclose his escape route but there was nothing he could do about it.

He jumped down. The shock of landing intensified the pain radiating from his ankle. He lay on the grass and waited until he had gathered his breath. He got up again.

The hours were ticking, and they might have been shortened drastically because of the visibility of the chipboard.

The country lane was quiet. He began limping along it. The hoverers were infrequent, and their passengers didn't seem to pay any attention to him. Nathan hoped that they wouldn't spot his blue hospital pyjamas.

Limping, he reached the first streetlights welcoming him to the village. There was a pub, and through the window he could see people drinking. They seemed happy. The bridge where the taxi Edgar had ordered was supposed to be waiting for him was about a mile's walk away if you followed the road. He passed the pub, and made a shortcut over the ditch and across the field.

Then he saw the searchlights.

The drones had been chasing the signal from his tag in the dark but now they had switched on their searchlights. They were less than hundred feet behind him and they had descended to a height of a few hundred feet.

The lights were for the robots that were about to get off the road and head toward his direction. He could see their blue uniforms in the street light.

The light titanium tag around his ankle began to feel heavy. It must have been rebooted straight after someone had discovered he had gone.

With the tag around his ankle he would never get away.

He started running, doing his best to ignore the pain that pierced his ankle like a twisted thorn. The robots behind him began to spread the net, the ones on the side moving super-fast in order to block his escape route.

The only escape route was the river ahead but he was still at least half a mile away from it. They were catching him fast and now not only the searchlights of the drones but also the headlights of the guard robots were firmly fixed on him.

At least he could now see the obstructions ahead.

He made it to the river bank with the robots only ten yards behind. There was no time to think; he slid down the bank and hit the shallow water.

The water was cold. He got deeper into the river and let the current carry him the moment the river was deep enough for his feet not to touch the bottom.

In seconds, he was nearly hundred yards downstream.

The robots didn't even try to follow him. They were unable to float. Instead, they began to run downstream.

The drones could keep the pace of the current and they hovered in the sky above him, following the signal from his tag.

He began to swim toward the opposite side of the river. The robots would cross the bridge and they would try to catch him on the other side.

He would have to get rid of the tag.

He managed to pull himself onto the riverbank and lay there, half of his body still in water, exhausted. The drones parked themselves above him.

There was a vital difference between the tags for inmates and patients. A patient could be held indefinitely but you couldn't fit him with an explosive tag.

Too many patients had killed themselves by hammering their tag until it had blown up. That's why the Human Rights Committee of the Solar Nations had banned them some years ago, so nowadays they were made of titanium and were impossible to unlock with brute force.

But he didn't need to do that.

He picked a large stone from the riverbank and began pummelling the titanium tag with it, trying to miss the swollen ankle.

Edgar had spotted the major design flaw in the tags. You needed special tools to remove it but you could break the broadcaster inside if you used force.

He didn't need to remove the tag. He only had to break the broadcaster.

He kept on hammering and hitting it in despair, until he realised that the searchlights were now moving away from him.

He looked up.

The drones were now drifting in the sky as if they had lost their purpose for existence.

They had other tracing mechanisms but they were still chasing the signal from the tag.

Only it wasn't there.

The robots ran nearer but they had lost their single-minded determination and looked like they were wandering around aimlessly.

He got back to the river.

The robots and the drones disappeared into the distance. He held onto the rock with all his strength. The exhaustion and the current tried to overpower him but he resisted the fatigue.

He still couldn't grasp why the thermal sensors of the robots hadn't spotted him. Perhaps they had been programmed to follow the signal from the tag only.

That was the trouble with programming robots. There was always a possibility for a blind spot, an unforeseen scenario, that little space that hadn't been covered by past experience, calculations, simulations, and the limited free will of the robots. Perhaps they had been programmed to ignore any other heat sources except the ones that came with the tag to ensure public safety.

Perhaps the programmers had wired them in such a way that they avoided deep water to the level that it overrode the mission to locate a fugitive.

In the end, a guard robot was still a major investment.

He made it back onto the riverbank, now another few hundred yards downstream, and lay there, until he gathered the strength to get up and limp to the bridge. The robot and drone search party were looking for him further downstream, probably calculating the speed of the current, and estimating his location based on that.

29.

The taxi was parked exactly where Edgar had said it would be but he wouldn't have discovered it had he not known where it was. Its stealth mode was on which made it completely unnoticeable to robotic eyes and barely invisible to humans.

It was an Underworld taxi and the robot chauffeur asked no questions, apart from his destination. He asked it to take him straight to Lola's house.

"Is there a first aid box?" he asked. A small compartment that he hadn't noticed came out in front of him. He saw a box of painkillers and took out two capsules which he forced down the throat.

The chauffeur must have noticed that he was wet as the heating went on. As the jolting pain from his ankle began to subside the heat lulled him asleep.

The chauffeur woke him up in front of Lola's house. It was still night. With the Midsummer Festival around the corner, the residents had left to the country and the street was nearly empty of hoverers.

The taxi left him standing in front of the house in dirty pyjamas.

It was a strange sight but a by-passer might have thought that he had been thrown out by a girlfriend after some domestic disturbance.

He hoped that Lola had not deactivated his guest key.

The door opened as normal and if Lola's security system was aware that he had been shut in a psychiatric institute for a long time, it didn't tell it.

She would be in bed, asleep. Edgar would have been wrong for the first time.

The screeching of the stairs welcomed him.

"Welcome home!" the security system chirped when he got to the door. "It has been a while since you have graced us with your presence!"

Who wrote all those cheesy lines? Was there a bloke somewhere whose only job was to prepare the automated systems for all eventualities or were they self-governing systems with capacity to invent new dialogue? Funny how his life was surrounded by machines and yet he had no idea about how they worked.

"Please keep the lights dim. And keep the shutters on! Also, could you please get me a cup of coffee?"

"Yes sir!"

Nathan had no idea who he was talking to. It was the time spent at the institute where the machines didn't respond to his commands but worked to keep him in that had made him aware of the dual nature of machines.

They were servants until they served someone else in which case they were well capable of killing and murdering you.

He knew straight away when he opened the door that Lola hadn't been home for days.

The apartment had a distinctive smell of her absence.

Nathan wondered if anyone was monitoring the apartment. If they did they would already be on their way.

He sat in the kitchen drinking coffee. His ankle was hurting again but right now he needed coffee more than the painkillers.

What had they mixed in the coffee at the institute? It had had a nasty aftertaste.

Even Edgar had been unable to fix that.

He limped to the bathroom and glanced at the mirror. He

looked as if he had been homeless in Mars for three months.

The face was scratched and it was half-covered with dried blood.

He took some painkillers and plunged into the bath. Then he took the black hair dye Lola kept in a bathroom drawer and applied it to his his hair.

He hoped Edgar would be alright. Edgar had loaded a bank account with a false name. The taxi driver had given him the wrist pad that connected to it. Edgar had been meticulous with every detail and he wondered whether the fact that no police had yet crashed in Lola's flat to arrest him had to do with some distraction Edgar had organised.

He took the first aid kit, and cleaned the bleeding ankle. Then he wrapped fresh bandage around it. He limped to Lola's bedroom and found his clothes in the wardrobe exactly where he had left them many months ago.

It was as if Lola had been expecting to get him back any day.

A pair of chinos and a white shirt. White boxing shoes that gave extra support to the ankle. Red socks. Blue underwear. Not the most fashionable of combinations but it had to do.

Now he had to find Lola.

Her scooter was parked outside. She never left far without it.

He checked the delivery data in the fridge. The last delivery had been made four days ago. She usually got orders in daily, as she liked to eat her veggies as fresh as possible.

He limped to the front room. The Yoruba jewellery that usually decorated the mantelpiece was missing.

That was a bad sign.

Nathan searched through the apartment for more clues. Her favourite pink travel case was there, so it seemed unlikely that she had travelled out of town, unless she had recently purchased a new one.

The last time she had used the suitcase had been three weeks and two days ago, to and back from a conference in Scarborough.

According to the central computer her next trip was due in three weeks to New York, and it already had a packing plan for the pink suitcase, yet to be authorised by Lola.

She hadn't bought a new one.

It seemed she had simply vanished. He called her wrist pad but only got the automated message which normally signified that someone was outside the reach of the AllNet—a near-technical impossibility if someone wore the wrist pad.

She had switched her wrist pad off or someone else had done that.

If Edgar had been right, she would be on her way to some undisclosed circle and about to be slaughtered by a bunch of bloodthirsty, ultraconservative druids.

One thing Edgar had not given any advice for was how to locate the circle she might have been taken to. It hadn't seemed like a glaring omission at the time but now he began to seriously wonder whether there had been a fundamental flaw in Edgar's plan.

What had been the point of escaping if there was no way to find Lola on time?

The next day was Midsummer and festival preparations would have begun all across Britain with hundreds of circles across the land preparing for an influx of devout members of the Order, the rest of the country celebrating the fact they had an extra holiday.

He searched the AllNet to see if his escape had become public knowledge but there was not even a rumour about his disappearance. That didn't necessarily mean anything as there were over five hundred thousand security cameras monitoring Greater London alone, all equipped with facial recognition software.

Voice recognition software could scan every AllNet conversation, and gods knew what other tools the police had in their arsenal.

All they had to do was to wait for him to appear somewhere and pick him up. There really wasn't any need for public manhunts.

Edgar had hacked into the Citizen Database and resurrected someone who was deceased. But very soon, an anomaly might be spotted and his false identity tracked down.

Thomas Hooper.

That was the name that came up on the wrist pad.

He would have to swap the new identity with another one, and keep on doing that for as long as he stayed under the jurisdiction of the Solar Nations.

Many criminals reportedly altered their identities every fifteen minutes but to achieve this frequency of identity alteration you needed some help, either from a corrupt official, or from a corrupt government in the Outworld.

But if they really wanted to find someone they would find a way.

The only way to get away from the government's clutches was to head to the Underworld, or the Outworld. Theoretically, you could also hide in the Home Planets but the tricky bit was to make it through the Customs.

In any case, he had to visit the Underworld. Also, he needed a reliable guide as he had to go much deeper than before.

It was now 9am. He made a call to Lola's office.

"Can I speak to Lola, please?" he asked once the receptionist picked the call.

"Unfortunately she's not in today," the receptionist answered.

"I work for the Martian Mining Corporation and we want to run a big campaign in the star cruiser. But I need to get hold of her before the festival, as the budgets won't be rolled over to the next quarter."

"She has been off sick for a few days. We're not expecting her in before the next week," the receptionist said.

"Sad to hear that. Is she recovering at home or at a hospital?"

"At home."

After he finished the call he put on a leather jacket, picked a pair of sun glasses, and limped downstairs. He glanced at his reflection in the mirror.

He could hardly recognise himself. He had never dyed his hair before, and the difference it made was striking.

Still, facial recognition software could probably see through his camouflage easily.

The street was busy with traffic. He walked to Lola's scooter and tried to open the storage case.

Fortunately, the scooter still recognised his retina, as his new identity on the wrist pad would have made the alarm scream. He pulled Lola's helmet out.

He could still smell her skin and perfume when he put the helmet on.

He switched the engine on and felt the uplift as the scooter rose up to two feet, its standby height. He pressed the accelerator gently.

The scooter took off and began to slide along the street. He rode slowly not only as he disliked riding, but also as there was no need to arouse any unnecessary attention.

He didn't need the traffic police chasing him right now.

As always, the narrow alleys of Chinatown were steaming hot. He parked the scooter in the underground parking near the entrance to the Underworld that led to the place of rendezvous where he had met with Snyder.

Snyder wasn't anywhere to be seen but he hadn't expected that. He only needed to get hold of someone who knew how to get hold of him.

He talked to the receptionist at the brothel opposite the room Snyder had used.

"Have you seen Snyder?"

"He hasn't been here for months," she said.

"Do you know how to get hold of him?"

"Snyder doesn't turn up to impromptu visits."

"I am a former customer. Normally I book an appointment but this time it's an emergency."

"There is a little shop down on the tenth level. They might know where he is. It doesn't mean that he would see you though."

"Thanks." He had to get hold of Snyder, as without the company of a local the Underworld respected it could be a pretty unwelcoming place.

There was a small chance that if he made it to the tenth level and Snyder wasn't there that he wouldn't make it up alive.

The old service lift took him down, and when he got out he realised that he had never been in the Underworld proper. The stink was a lot stronger than on the upper levels, and he had to sidestep the puddle of oil straight in front of the lift.

On the upper levels everything had been reasonably tidy and light. It was a lot dimmer here in the lower levels.

But the real difference were the people. Even the receptionist of the whorehouse had seemed relatively normal with her minuscule metallic eyebrow implants.

He had heard about the Freaks who believed that man should have been made of metal and blades rather than flesh and bones, and that gods had made a design mistake.

He had never met one before.

Or the Bards who had been trying to metamorphose into musical instruments for decades. Walking along the first corridor, he encountered a whole orchestra of them.

They didn't need to carry any instruments.

They were the instruments, and as they breathed, they made music.

There were a lot of Underworlders with animal implants.

He made it to the shop undisturbed although some of the Underworlders stared at him as if he were the worst freak of them all.

The shop was an old comic store that still sold printed comic books. The shopkeeper dressed up like Donald Duck the Zombie.

"I've heard that you might know where Snyder is," Nathan said.

The shopkeeper said nothing.

The door opened and closed behind. He turned around to see two huge, nasty-looking Freaks standing there.

"So you are looking for Snyder," the first one said.

"Yes."

"The last one who looked for him is dead."

"I am an old customer."

"Snyder doesn't talk to anyone from the Overworld nowadays."

"I really need his help. I'm willing to pay as much as he likes to charge."

"Sorry. You're lucky to get out of here alive."

"He is a fugitive," the shopkeeper said.

"I knew I had seen him somewhere," the Freak said. "The lunatic chief druid's son. Perhaps we shouldn't let him go after all. That bastard and his family have inflicted so much trouble on us."

His camouflage didn't seem effective at all.

"He saved Neeta's life," the shopkeeper added. "I don't think you want to incur her wrath."

"Maybe he isn't as bad as his family. Ok. I'll take him to Snyder."

The two Freaks turned around and left the shop. Nathan followed them.

The Freaks moved fast, navigating through the maze of collapsed corridors, broken elevators, pools of oil, rubbish and dark stairways. All Nathan knew was that they were moving deeper and deeper into the Underworld. There was no way that he could ever make it back up without a guide. No wrist pad navigation system worked here. And step after step, the air was getting hotter.

It was becoming harder and harder for him to breathe. But the Freaks kept on moving fast.

After about half an hour's trek they stopped by a narrow door in a corridor that looked more like a part of a residential district although there had been corner shops selling gigantic, fried rats and mice nearby.

It occurred to him that perhaps the diet of the Underworlders wasn't quite the same than his.

The smaller Freak pressed an old-fashioned buzzer at the door. Around half a minute later Snyder slid the door open.

"Look who's that!" he said when he saw Nathan. "You don't know the trouble you got me in."

Snyder led them inside and pointed toward a worn sofa. Nathan sat down.

"After I did that job for you I have been chased by cops and nearly killed by some hit man. Thankfully the Overworlders hardly know their way around here. But I have had to keep on moving."

"Sorry about that."

"You have pissed off some influential people and they have access to high-tech resources. But I know how to play cat and mouse a lot better than them. Down here, their resources don't have much use. Want some coffee?"

Snyder didn't wait for an answer but poured some black liquid from a pot into a metal mug. He passed the mug to Nathan.

"It isn't quite as good as the stuff up there," he said. "The beans have been grown under artificial light."

Nathan tasted the drink. It wasn't nearly as disgusting as he had feared.

"So what brought you here?" Snyder asked. "And how did you get out of the institute?"

"I had some help. But I need you to do another hacking job for me."

"My equipment was trashed by some thugs."

"It isn't an easy job either. I need you to hack into someone's personal memory. Someone I must find before it's too late. "

"That's nearly impossible."

"Can you do it?"

"The people who are after you are evil. They tortured a receptionist to death just because she didn't give the information about my whereabouts quickly enough. I'd do anything to make them pay for that. Who do you want to find?"

"Her name is Lola."

"I see. It might take a while."

"How long?"

"A couple of hours. Three days. Who knows. These systems are supposed to be un-hackable. But there's always a way."

Snyder vanished to the back room. All Nathan could do was wait. And drink the coffee.

Three hours later Snyder came back.

"Any luck?"

"I found her. She's in Cloud 913. You'll only get one look, for five minutes or less. After that, the anti-hacking trawlers will severe the connection. You need to pick those five minutes very carefully, as all you have is raw data from her stream of consciousness. Basically, you will see and feel what she saw and felt during those five minutes."

"Can we get real-time data about where she is? Right now."

"Unfortunately not. Based on the mapping of the cloud, it seems that she has been in a sedated state for nearly a week. Also, her wrist pad is only giving basic information now. Nothing like the coordinates of where she is. It seems that her state might have been caused by some medication. I can't poke deeper into the cloud without alerting the trawlers. The best bit would be focusing on the last five minutes before she lost her consciousness. Perhaps you will be able to see the person who abducted her."

"How do you know that she has been abducted?"

Snyder looked at him and for a second sympathy flickered in his eyes. Then it vanished.

"I'll leave you to it," he said and left the room.

Nathan had thought that there would be a helmet or glasses or something that he should put on, but there was no technical equipment.

His wrist pad beeped once. It was downloading something. Abruptly, a new visual reality broke into his consciousness.

He was in the back of a hoverer. The windows were darkened. He tried to move his hands but they were tied together. Inside him, something kicked like a terrified foetus, sensing the mother's horror and wanting to run.

Only it couldn't.

The two Nigerians in front were chatting but he couldn't hear the words. He wanted to vomit. It felt like morning sickness on steroids.

The hoverer drove fast along the country lane. Then it began to slow down.

It stopped and parked in front of a country cottage.

The third man sitting next to him took out a needle from his bag and injected it in his arm. He couldn't resist.

"Time to sleep," he said.

The last thing he saw before losing consciousness was someone coming out of the cottage.

It was Morris Chapman.

Then he was back in the room.

Snyder had come back.

"Any luck?"

"I know where they took her. I know who took her."

"Good. Before you leave you need to get your ankle back in shape. I know an Underworld surgeon that can get it fixed in no time. Also, you need to get the tag removed."

Three hours later Nathan was on his way up. Snyder gave him a rucksack with some equipment, weapons and more wrist pads. He also handed him a tennis-ball-sized device. It had a singular red button.

"This is a gift. Use this only in emergency. It works only once. It has been synchronised with your DNA. Everyone else but you will feel dizzy and will be knocked out for two minutes. Hopefully, enough time for you to escape with her."

"What is it?"

"You don't want to hear the technical explanation. Let's just say that its pulsation interferes with the work of your blood cells. But the effects are only temporary."

"One of the Freaks said that my father has inflicted horrendous pain on the Underworld. What did he mean?"

"You shouldn't ask questions you don't want to hear an answer to."

It was late afternoon and Nathan headed straight out of London. The ride to Morris' cottage would take for a while and there was no guarantee that Lola would even be there. In fact it was unlikely that she would, as the preparations for the Midsummer Festival the next day were long underway. But at least there could be some clues left behind.

He had time to look into Guinevere's death and Lola's abduction on the way.

He projected his wrist pad screen on the visor of the helmet and went straight to the official AllNet residence of the Order. It housed an extensive, albeit skewed historical and linear model of the development of the stone circles.

He wasn't looking for that.

At the institute, he had had time to think quite a bit about Guinevere's death.

What had bothered him most was that she should have been killed at one of the stone circles.

But most stone circles were tourist attractions and hundreds of people would gather at them especially during the druid festivals such as Midsummer.

But the druids fanatical enough to commit ritual killings wouldn't compromise on the location. They would want to commit their atrocious acts at a shrine whose history would go beyond the mists of time.

The more ancient the shrine, the better. But the oldest of the shrines were also the most popular tourist destinations and hardly the places where to commit ritual murders.

How did you conceal an ancient stone circle?

By erasing it from the map and all religious literature. By erasing even footnotes to it from history.

Had he had the time he would have gone straight to Foyles, to the bookstore's records that were disconnected from the AllNet as they had never been part of it. Because they had never been digitised they could not have been digitally altered. But he had the second best thing.

He would have to go through maps drawn before the Abolition of the Human Sacrifice Act. And what he had seen in the basement of Morris Chapman's cottage made him confident that it would be the place to find just that.

There had been a copy of a map drawn by Hubert O'Cannaghan, one of the first scholars to take a more scientific perspective in the study of the old British religion, and mapped all the stone circles in Britain over five hundred years ago.

That was well before the abolition, before the time the human sacrifice went underground.

As he expected, Morris Chapman's cottage looked vacated. He parked his scooter behind the cottage and peeked in through the kitchen window. No one was in.

He broke the window with his elbow and listened. He could hear no sounds coming from the house. No alarm. He lifted the window pane up and climbed in.

The door to the basement was locked but he was able to force it in. It seemed obvious that Morris Chapman relied on the protection from someone high up in the Order and that the real reasons behind his departure from the police force would have been totally different than the ones mentioned in the headlines.

Maybe all these years he had worked as a bait. For anyone like Guinevere and him who would be curious enough to look into the inexplicable deaths but cautious enough to not trust anyone. A discredited, retired police investigator obsessed with ancient ritual killings would in those circumstances fit the bill of a trustworthy-looking individual.

Or perhaps he had been hiding as he worked as a problem solver for the fundamentalist druids. He had a feeling that he would probably find out soon but he wasn't sure if he would survive the discovery.

Hubert O'Cannaghan's map was where he had left it months ago.

There had been rumours about human sacrifices in the archeological circles for years, albeit the Order had always stated that even before the Abolition of the Human Sacrifice Act the killings had always been committed by insane individuals or serial killers. But with the Order tightly controlling access to its archives and claiming that they contained too much personal information to be made public—and with a significant majority of pro-Order MPs in the Parliament blocking any legislation to open the archives—it was impossible to verify the truth value of their statement.

Three years ago, a mummified body of a young woman had been found in a bog fifty yards from a disused stone circle near Oxford, bearing the signs of a violent death and possibly, ritual murder. According to carbon dating, she had died around three hundred years ago.

At Avebury Circle, buried in a dig designed for one of the megaliths, someone had found a skeleton of a three-year-old boy, murdered around twenty-one years ago.

But both the academics and the police were looking for conclusive evidence. There were enough clues pointing at the direction of ritual murders but you needed a significant level of distrust in authority to be able to connect the dots.

30.

It was early morning. He had been comparing Hubert O'Cannaghan's map with contemporary maps through the night. Someone had rung the bell around 10pm but gone away, leaving him to wait in anxiety, hoping that whoever it was wouldn't walk around the cottage and find the scooter.

He had listened and waited quietly for half an hour but there were no more sounds.

He had narrowed down the potential sites to fifteen locations, all within two hundred miles from London. There were many more further away but based on where Guinevere and his mother had been found he was certain that this wasn't some sort of Highlands splinter group. No, these druids wouldn't get too far from London.

The trouble was that fifteen was fourteen too many.

He didn't have enough time to eliminate the wrong locations by relying on luck.

He had to try to establish why the individual circles had been taken off the map.

They could have fallen in disrepair and been removed from the Order's maps due to health and safety regulations. He did a quick AllNet scan but found no reference to any of the fifteen locations. But then, ten out of fifteen had been in an area that had clearly been taken over by residential buildings.

It was unlikely that none of them existed anymore.

That left five possibilities. Three out of five were too far away from him and he reckoned them in any case to be historically too insignificant to be used by anyone in a major clan.

That left two circles.

One of the circles was twenty miles north from where he was, another eighty miles east.

As Lola had been brought to the cottage it would make sense for the circle to be not too far away.

He would be able to visit these two spots before midnight but that would use all his time.

What troubled him was that these derelict circles had no apparent link to the family. Based on their names, they were linked to clans that had fallen from power into obscurity hundreds of years ago. That explained their poor state, as if the clan wasn't there to look after the circle no one would maintain it.

There had to be something with more significance nearby, a location more fitting to a clan with the stature of McKinleys. Nathan glanced over the map for historical landmarks that didn't have a circle marked next to them.

The ruins of Wardour Castle were nearby.

The castle had been built around eight hundred years ago by Lord Wigmore, a veteran of the Hundred Years' War. The outer wall was hexagonal with a gatehouse to the north. The bailey and castle were also hexagonal. The castle had two towers. Two hundred years later the castle had undergone major reconstruction work, and the narrow medieval windows had been replaced with large Gothic ones. Twenty years later, the family, royalists, had been besieged by the parliamentarians. They had taken the castle. Six months later the royalists had taken the castle back but only after they had inflicted severe damage. Later on, it had been used as a set for many Robin Hood flat films. Those had been the days when the filmmakers actually built sets and used locations.

But there were no records of stone circles ever having been there.

Lord Wigmore had been a druid and he had had sinister reputation. Villagers had vanished, and there were wild tales about what had happened to them. What was certain was that bodies had there been many, and even if you put down the numbers to exaggeration and stories about macabre ways of dying to medieval superstition, there was still enough material for at least some factual deaths.

Isabel had often talked about the castle. It was from Isabel that he had heard the ghost stories about headless corpses dancing on the moors, their skulls flying in the air, and the ghosts of the dead little children appearing to people. They said that the whole region was haunted, cursed due to the innocent blood that had been spilled over the ground over hundreds of years.

He had been an ancestor.

He decided that Wardour Castle would be the best bet.

He looked at the maps again. Was there anything around the castle that could hide a stone circle?

An ancient grove, a protected preservation area perhaps?

According to the modern maps there was an area that was off-limits to the general public as it was one of the last natural habitations of wild-growing bluebell in Britain.

That looked promising.

An hour and a half later he parked Lola's scooter at the castle's parking area.

Wardour Castle was a tourist attraction, and even during the Midsummer there were some Japanese tourists walking around the castle.The tourist office and parts of the castle seemed closed.

The last few hundred years hadn't been kind to the castle.

Even in daylight it looked like a dark, unwelcoming corpse of a castle, its stones eroded by the sun, rain, hail, wind and the wide range of ammunition shot at it over the centuries.

Nathan wondered what the Japanese tourists were doing there

as there was nothing to see, as most of the castle was closed. But it didn't look like the castle would be much busier in a normal day.

There was a hired hoverer in front of the castle from Budget Hoverer, the one the Japanese must have had brought.

The tourists were the only sign of life. The bluebell area turned out to be a false lead as it turned out to be just a bluebell area.

He looked at the map. There was a little road that began behind the castle. It seemed to lead nowhere, ending abruptly around half a mile from the castle.

Why had the road been built if it led nowhere?

He got on top of the scooter, and rode around the castle. The Japanese tourists were now standing on the half-destroyed wall and taking pictures.

He waved at them. They smiled and waved back.

A narrow dirt road, covered with weeds led toward a grove. It looked like no one had driven it for years. But then, hoverers didn't leave many traces. Floating few feet above the road, they didn't need to care about the weeds.

Perhaps the derelict state of the castle area was designed to deceive the visitors to think that no one ever came there.

Or perhaps no one ever came there.

But he had a distinct feeling that if someone was trying to hide a stone circle, it was done remarkably well.

The lane became narrower. Although the engine was nearly noise-free he revved it down.

Then the road ended. There was a thick forest ahead. He stopped the scooter. He could hear no sounds apart from the natural sounds of the forest.

He took the rucksack from the back of the scooter and began to walk through the undergrowth.

Even when it was late afternoon it was still scorching hot and the mosquitoes and flies buzzing around were clearly attracted to his sweat.

He had been walking for few minutes when he came to an opening.

There were derelict stones of an ancient circle ahead.

After another minute of walking he made it to the circle.

It was instantly clear that no one had maintained the site for years. That wasn't a good sign. For all their secrecy, human sacrifices would always take place somewhere reasonably well looked after, for the simple reason that religious people always liked to take care for their altars.

He looked at the stones more closely. They had faint but clearly visible carvings of human skulls and bones. That was unusual, as normally the stones were bare and had no artwork. Perhaps Lord Wigmore had indeed committed a few ritual murders.

But it hardly mattered.

He had followed a false lead. Lola had never been here.

He sat on a broken stone in despair.

Then he looked at the skeletons and skulls again. He had seen similar ones before.

"Oh my gods!"

It was 8.15pm. He had less than four hours to make it to Oxford and come up with a war plan on the way.

It was 11.29pm when he stopped the hoverer by a side road not too far from the old house. Although he lived in Oxford he hadn't been there after he had visited it once around seven years ago.

Too many memories of Mum.

The front garden was exactly how he remembered it, well-kept and colourful, but there were around a dozen hoverers parked in front of the house.

He had made a small excursion home, taking the risk of getting caught in case anyone monitored it, and picked the druid costume he had worn at Guinevere's funeral.

Now it was time to put the robe on.

His plan was entirely based on no one having removed the little adjustment Mum had made to the security system when he had been a little boy. She had asked him to keep quiet about it, and at the time he had thought that she had done it because she had wanted to ensure that Nathan could get in, no matter what.

Now he suspected that she had been scared for her life, and wanted to ensure that he would be able to get out, if necessary.

She had given him full housemaster's credentials. A routine scan of the system would not have revealed it, but if it had been scanned by security professionals, it could have been found.

"Nice to see you Nathan, after such a long time," the door said and slid open.

"Don't tell anyone I'm here," he said.

It was in the corridor when he became certain that he had arrived at the right place.

The live fires were burning in the fireplaces, welcoming the visitors.

The beat of the druid drum sounded familiar and yet different from what he remembered it to have been at the numerous Midsummer Festivals he had attended.

The beat was distinctly African.

He had visited the basement once when he had been four or five.

The carvings of the skeleton men had welcomed him in the stairs. He hadn't been superstitious then and he wasn't superstitious now but he had never made it any further.

Whatever it had been that was hidden in the basement, it oozed such evil that he didn't want to know more about it.

This time, the door was locked.

"Open," he said. And it did.

When he opened the door, the beat of the African drum became louder. He could now hear the humming of the druids in the distance.

He covered his face with a hood.

He walked the stairs down. There was a closed door at the bottom of the stairs but it seemed disconnected from the security system. He opened it and peeked in.

How do you hide an ancient stone circle in Oxford?

You build a house over it.

The whole basement was just open space with a stone circle in the middle.

The archaeologist in him hardly saw the druids who seemed too preoccupied by their worship to notice that yet another druid had joined them. In the end, no one would be expecting any uninvited guests.

In the mythology of the Order there had been the first stone circle ever built on the British Isles but its location had been lost. It made sense; one of the hundreds of stone circles must have been built first. Consequently, the many older stone circles around the island claimed that glory.

Nathan had a distinct feeling that he had just found what could be the first stone circle in Britain. And all those years he had been living over it.

Unlike all the other stone circles he had seen in Britain, this circle resembled the African stone circles he had seen in Nabta Playa. But this one wasn't derelict.

There were about twenty druids dancing around the circle and although they were all hooded it was obvious which ones were African as the rest of the druids danced rather clumsily.

At the centre of the circle there was an altar. At the altar, there was Lola. She was naked.

And visibly pregnant.

She was waking up from a drug-induced sleep. Just like Guinevere would have done.

It was 11.47pm. She had thirteen minutes to live.

He could see the blurred horror in her eyes as she began to realise what was happening. She tried to move but the leather cords kept her tied to the altar.

The druids, sensing blood, started chanting even louder, and the drumbeat became nearly unbearably loud.

In the action films he had seen, the hero would always end up spoiling the surprise and giving the opposition a chance to respond. The situation would escalate but the hero would save the day.

The truth was that he wouldn't walk out of the basement alive with Lola if he gave the druids a chance. Each druid had their dagger, and they wouldn't hesitate to use it. There were simply too many of them.

Now it wasn't the time to play a hero. He took the little device Snyder had given to him and pressed the button.

All druids but one began to stumble and fell on the floor.

The one druid left standing turned around and faced him. He pulled a dagger from the waist pocket and walked toward him.

It was Edward.

"Uncle," Nathan said. "I am going to take her with me. You'd better move out of the way. Otherwise I'll have to kill you."

"No you won't. I'll kill you first."

He had half a minute to get Lola out of the basement before the rest of the druids would regain their consciousness.

He had no time to waste.

He pulled the handgun out of his pocket and aimed at his uncle's head.

Then he pulled the trigger.

The bullet hit his uncle in the face and tore half of it apart.

His uncle flew backwards and fell on the floor.

He picked a dagger one of the druids had dropped on the floor and ran toward the altar.

He cut the leather cords quickly and lifted Lola on his shoulder.

She seemed completely disoriented, as she had been affected by the device as badly as everyone else.

He took a quick glance around and saw one of the druids getting up. He kicked him in the face with a karate kick.

The druid hit the floor, and blood spilled on the floor.

He didn't really have to do that. But he had wanted to do that.

He carried Lola up the stairs and shut the door behind. Then he made it to the front door.

"Initiate the emergency shutdown procedure," Nathan said to the door.

"Yes, sir," the door responded.

By the time Nathan had made it to the scooter, all the windows and doors of the house had been shut down.

It would take them at least twenty minutes to get out of the house, enough time for him to make it out of Oxford.

He now turned his attention to Lola. She was now fully awake. She was sobbing.

"It's alright," he said. "I'm here."

She recognised him.

"Nathan!" she said. "I thought I would never see you again!"

"We need to leave now. You need to be strong for the scooter ride."

It was hot but Lola was shivering.

He took off his robe and put it on Lola. Then he lifted her on top of the scooter. He helped her put the helmet on.

Lola wrapped her arms around him. He turned the scooter around, accelerated, and left.

In the gardens around, the fires were lit, welcoming the new season.

Fireworks blew up in the sky.

Two people on a scooter, one wearing nothing else but a druid's robe would have been a weird sight any other night, but on the way to London they saw people that looked a lot stranger than that. The Midsummer night was always a strange night, and on the way to London they passed wild roadside druid parties, Japanese tourist groups reliving the 'first' Midsummer party, probably being ripped off in the process, and extraordinarily, even folks that seemed completely sober.

31.

Nathan felt Lola's body on the back. She had held onto him through the ride as if there were no tomorrow. The streets were still half-full of revellers but the slowly humming road-wiping robots had already appeared to do the hard work of bringing Britain back to normalcy from yet another Midsummer Festival. By the morning all the rubbish would have disappeared from the streets.

It took another ten minutes to ride to Chinatown from West London. He parked the scooter in front of the Japanese whorehouse he had visited when he had been looking for Snyder and paid for a room. The Underworld proper would have been a better place to hide but it had its own dangers.

This way no one would be asking any questions.

He half-walked, half-carried Lola up the stairs, shut the door of the room behind, and they both fell asleep on the bed. When he woke up in the afternoon Lola was still asleep.

He lay there and watched her. Even when she was covered in dirt, without any makeup and dressed up in an ill-fitting druid robe, she still looked like the most beautiful woman in the galaxy.

By the time he had come back from the shower she had woken up.

"You don't give in easily," she said. "And before get any wrong ideas, the baby is yours."

"Edgar told me that much."

He put his hand on her stomach. The baby kicked.

"It is saying hello to Dad!" she said.

"You must be starving. Let me get something to eat."

"I still feel like I want to vomit. They will come after us. Where will we go?"

"I don't know. We will hide in the Underworld for a while. I have some contacts there. Then we'll try to make it to the Outworld. They won't give us rest as long as we stay in the Solar Nations."

Nathan gave her the clothes he had taken from her apartment and she dressed up.

The red walls of the room had paintings of naked people having sex, some of them stretched in ways beyond Nathan could imagine a human body could flex. Not all the paintings depicted people but there were also robots and half-people. This was hardly a place to bring a fine young lady.

He could hear footsteps in the corridor. Then the door opened.

Morris Chapman came in, followed by the two Nigerian men Nathan had fought in Lola's apartment. They carried guns.

"Hate to interrupt the reunion," Morris said.

"Here comes the serial killer," Nathan said.

"I'm just a hired hand."

The two Africans handcuffed Nathan and Lola. They were escorted downstairs, and outside.

The black Mercedes was waiting for them. The Africans pushed them on the back seat.

They drove out of London. An hour later they passed a small village. The hoverer began to slow down. It turned left to a narrow private road and then came to a farm. The hoverer stopped in front of the farmhouse.

The black men got out of the hoverer and forced Nathan and Lola out. They stood in front of the farmhouse and waited.

Another hoverer approached the farmhouse.

It stopped next to the black Mercedes.

Two people came out.

Dad and Edward.

Or what was left of Edward. Half of Edward's face was gone, revealing the metallic frame of a cyborg.

"Sad to see you in these unfortunate circumstances," Dad said.

"It is your action that has made them unfortunate," Nathan said.

"Look at what you did to your uncle," Dad said, ignoring Nathan's comment. "Or what used to be your uncle," he added. "It'll take a lot of money to fix that."

Edward stared at him with the right eye like a cyclops.

"What have you made of him?" Nathan asked. It dawned on him that Edward's robotic stiffness had been rather—robotic.

"He inflicted that on himself. I saved him. Now, let's get to business."

"Did you kill Mum yourself or was it one of your cronies?"

"I didn't do it."

"But you benefited from it. That's why you are the chief druid today."

"I can't deny that."

"So this is what the Order is today. A body-part harvesting ring masquerading as a religion."

"And you are the people behind the kidnapping and killing of kids in Africa," Lola said. "May your soul rot in Hades!"

"Only if Hades exists. Besides, your African brothers are well capable of running the organ harvesting business by themselves."

"And you're ready to murder your own grandchild," Lola said. "After you have murdered your own wife. Just to gain some extra years on Earth."

"For what it's worth, I never have planned to kill my grandchild."

"So what was this all about?" Lola asked. "Did you just plan to kill me?"

"Your foetus would never become my grandchild because Nathan isn't my son. I am not as coldblooded as you think. Yes, I approved the killing of his mother. But that was because I found out that he had slept with another man. And Nathan was the end result of that long-term adulterous relationship."

Everything Nathan believed to be true about his past had just been altered. And yet he felt numb. What Michael had just said explained everything. It made perfect sense.

"So you killed her as an act of revenge."

"Yes and no. After I found out that she had slept with Edward she became expedient."

Nathan glanced at Edward who was just standing there.

"Yes. But it was really about paying for the transgressions of her clan. And they couldn't find any volunteers. So we chose her. Perhaps the fact that she had betrayed me played a part in that."

"And what about Edward? What happened to him?"

"He couldn't remain silent. I still cared for him, so I let him live. In the end, I couldn't kill my brother. I am not a monster. But we were in the process of developing cyborg technology. Also, I thought it could be useful to have an ally in the Parliament."

"So you turned him into a half-human, half-machine."

"Better that than dead. At least he has the best shot out of us to live forever."

Nathan felt sick. But he wanted to know what had happened. This was his one shot at knowing the truth.

"And Guinevere?"

"Isabel wants to live forever as well."

"So you were behind the bombing in the train."

"I guess there is no point in denying it."

"You have been asking all the questions," Morris interrupted. "Somebody helped you escape from the institute. Who?"

"I like to keep some things a mystery."

"We'll find that soon enough."

"Time to go," Michael said. "I need to get a speech written

that explains why my son escaped only to butcher his pregnant girlfriend. I'll leave you to Morris and Edward's capable hands."

He turned around and climbed in the hoverer.

"Let the fun begin," Morris said.

When Nathan woke up he was soaked in sweat. The back compartment of the hoverer where they had been taken after Morris had injected them with something that had put them to sleep didn't have air-conditioning, and the afternoon sun had made it into a sauna.

His throat felt dry and rough like the surface of a sandpapering robot, and he badly needed a drink.

He felt Lola's body next to him. She was still asleep. It was pitch black so he couldn't see her but at least she was breathing.

They were still handcuffed. It seemed that this time these thugs didn't take any risks.

After about half an hour the hoverer stopped. A door opened and closed. Then the compartment door opened, and the smaller Nigerian peeked in.

"I can see you are awake here," he said and grinned. "This will be so much more fun when you know what is going on."

Edward's half-face looked in. The Nigerian thug and Edward pulled them out of the hoverer.

Lola was waking up.

The larger Nigerian who had been waiting for them was dressed in a white surgical suit and rubber gloves.

Nathan could see horror building on Lola's face, as she was coming to terms with the fact that for the second time in twenty-four hours she had woken up to be butchered. The Nigerian in the surgeon's suit smiled broadly when he saw Lola's face.

"I'll ensure that the harvesting will be trouble-free. In a way, it is better to do it today when we don't need to worry about all the religious stuff related to the Midsummer Festival. Your bits will all be fresh, so there will be no decrease in quality."

"So that's what your religion is at its purest. Only a way to harvest organs so that some wealthy Nigerian will be able to live another twenty years," Nathan said.

"You'll have to die anyway because of what you know. Isn't it nice to know that your life will benefit others, even after your death?" the Nigerian said.

They were deep in a dense forest. No one would hear their screams.

Another hoverer approached. It landed next to the black Mercedes. Morris Chapman came out.

"Now the freezer unit is here," the smaller Nigerian said. "We're ready to go. It's time for the last rites."

The other Nigerian began pushing them down a little-used pathway that led deeper in the forest. After about five minutes of walking he could see a stone circle ahead.

They were taken to the centre of the circle.

"Kneel," Edward said.

Nathan and Lola knelt down.

"You'll be glad to know that the ritual murder of your girlfriend will be solved quickly, as both the murderer and the weapon will be found at the scene of the killing," Morris said. "Unfortunately, you didn't want to live after cutting her open and pulling out the unborn foetus and her internal organs. And eating them. "

"At least we'll spend our last moments together," Lola said.

"I'm really sorry that I dragged you into all this," Nathan whispered.

Morris Chapman and the surgeon stood next to him.

The other Nigerian was wheeling a large freezer unit toward them.

"Why don't they make these things into robots?" he asked, struggling with the weight.

"The party is about to start," the surgeon said.

He pulled a surgeon's knife out of his bag.

"I wouldn't do that if I were you."

That was Stephen's voice. What was he doing here?

Morris and the Nigerian turned around.

"And what will you do to obstruct it?" Morris asked.

"Stephen!" Edward said. "Please don't interfere with this."

"No one needs to get hurt," Stephen responded. "Not if you let Nathan and Lola leave with me. Alive."

"Walk away, son, and forget what you have seen."

"Sorry. I can't do that."

"I'll kill you if I have to."

"Brit was faithful to you to the very end. They tortured her but she never gave out your name. It was Isabel who betrayed you."

"I don't believe you." Momentarily, what was left of Edward's face appeared to be in deep pain.

"Enough of family issues! We need to get on with this. Ade, you deal with Stephen. He's alone after all."

The surgeon placed the knife on Lola's throat.

The other Nigerian pulled a handgun from his pocket. He aimed it at Stephen.

"Sorry to kill you after just being introduced to you," he said.

Edward kicked Morris in the head. Morris fell.

Nathan had no idea about how Edward's feet had been fortified but Morris' head had burst open like a ripe melon.

Then Edward pulled out a handgun and faster than Nathan could follow, he shot at the surgeon and Ade in the head.

Then he fell.

It seemed that he was dead before he had even hit the ground.

Nathan got up.

Stephen searched through Morris' pockets until he found the key to the handcuffs.

Then he released Nathan and Lola.

Nathan looked over Edward's body.

"Sorry you never knew he was your Dad," Stephen said.

"Sorry that you lost yours."

"Nothing to be sorry about. There was not much left of him. I lost him years ago."

"What happened? How did he die so fast? And why did he change his mind?"

"Edgar short-circuited his system. It was enough to liberate his mind for a brief moment from the shackles it had been in. But that short-circuiting also destroyed him, as his mind had been on life support since they made him what he became. He is now free from the torture of having to do what he detested doing."

Nathan wrapped his arms around Lola who was still shivering from the aftershock of yet another near-death experience.

"How did you find us?" he asked.

"By tapping into the same tag that they used to find you. Your friends in the Underworld couldn't find that one. Not their fault, really, as it was only activated after you found Lola. Let's go now."

"What about the bodies?"

The Order will do the cover-up. They are a lot better in that than us."

"Who do you work for, Stephen?"

"I guess there is no point in hiding the facts anymore. You have probably guessed that I am a member of the Circle."

"So the Circle is for real."

"Of course."

"Why do you let these things happen? Why haven't you ever risen up against the Order? Exposed what they do?"

"There are many reasons. First and foremost, we aren't strong enough. We did stop the public ritual killings but monitoring each druid of the Order isn't that easy. We simply don't have the resources for it. But we are also a pacifist and democratic organisation, and using force has to be sanctioned by the gathering. And in recent years, it has been nearly impossible to arrange any of them, especially as the Order is now using security services to track down the members of the Circle as potential terrorists. That's why they blew up the train. They wanted to legalise special anti-terrorist measures so that they could use unlimited force against us."

"Is there any way to bring them down?"

"Evil has always existed in the world. Our resources are limited and we can't risk being found out.That's why we focus on macro-managing the big picture rather than micro-management. If we can affect the big picture, perhaps one day the universe will be inhabited by peace-loving societies that abhor violence rather than wield the sword. But this society isn't ready yet. After all, the body-part trade is what runs this world and nearly everyone pretends not to know about it."

"So how are Lola and I part of the big picture?"

"We don't know it yet. But one way or other, you are."

They were now approaching Stephen's hoverer. Its back door opened and Edgar wheeled out.

"Nice to see you in good shape, sir."

"How did you get him out so quickly?"

"After your escape, we sent the police to gather your belongings for forensic investigation. One of them works for us."

"So what will happen to us?" Lola asked.

"You will disappear into the galaxy. I'll be travelling on board *55 Cancri 1* in a week's time. We will provide you with new identities and you will travel with me. I don't think that the Order will bother to hunt you down in space, even if they found out where you are."

"So you are asking us to leave our life behind," Lola said.

"You already have. It isn't as if the Order will let you live and tell the world what you have seen."

Stephen got on the front seat. "You will stay in a little country cottage overnight until we get your identities sorted out. Your new names will be Ethan and Melissa Hanes. I took the liberty of getting you married—on paper. I hope you don't mind that."

"Ethan and Melissa Hanes." Lola sounded the names out.

"I could get used to them," she said.

"Those are the best names I could get. But their original owners won't be coming back to reclaim them anytime soon."

32.

Stephen took them to a country cottage around fifty miles from the coastal town of New Brighton where the dock for the shuttle that would transport them to 55 *Cancri 1* was located. The City of Brighton had been wiped out by a tsunami and the lot smaller town of New Brighton had been chosen as the location of the dock to symbolise new beginnings.

The new wrist pads configured for their new identities would be delivered shortly.

It was Edgar that had, discreetly, gathered all the necessary data for that.

It was a medieval cottage with fireplaces and no electricity. Edgar lit the fireplaces to heat up the place and then it left with Stephen.

It still had to file a witness' testimony about Nathan's escape.

They went to sleep straight away. When Nathan woke up the fire had burnt the wood. It was 4.12am and still dark. Nathan put some new wood to the fireplace and lit it.

He noticed that someone had put their new wrist pads on the table. They had slept so tight that he hadn't even woken up to a visit by the delivery robot.

This was his first day as Ethan Hanes. When he came back, Lola was still asleep but she mumbled something sleepily when he shook the bed accidentally.

"Sorry. I didn't mean to wake you up."

She pulled close to him and held him sleepily. Nathan waited until she had fallen asleep again, and then he got out of the bed. He couldn't sleep but sat on the couch, watching Lola breathe, and was grateful to be alive. Even under the duvet, her bump stood up.

He was going to be a father. Although he was happy about it, that was a lot to take.

He wasn't quite sure whether he was ready for it but he was grateful that at least, the mother was Lola. He promised to himself that somewhere along the line, they would have a proper wedding.

Lola opened her eyes and saw him staring at her.

"What?"

"Nothing. Just sleep. Sleep tight."

Nathan opened the parcel containing the wrist pads. Inside, there were two portals, one for Ethan and one for Melissa, and two small cases, again one for Ethan and one for Melissa. He opened his case. Inside, there were two devices, one with a shape of a glove, another one resembling sunglasses.

These were the basic tools for the change of identity.

He put on the gloves which began to alter his fingerprints. Ten minutes later the unique fingerprints of Nathan McKinley were gone and he had become Ethan.

He suspected that somehow Edgar would also have found a way of breaking into the Central DNA Database of the Solar Nations and reallocated Nathan's unique DNA fingerprint to Ethan.

Next he put the glasses on and kissed his blue eyes goodbye. He could not feel anything but fifteen minutes later when he took of the glasses his eyes were green. Edgar had explained why they didn't just tamper the global database and kept the colour and the unique pattern of his eyes and fingerprints.

That basic-level identity recognition data was available to banks, libraries, government institutions, and so on, and it would have been impossible to touch all these databases without at least leaving an anomaly somewhere, and that anomaly would have been discovered by the trawlers at some stage.

Lola's new pupils had the colour of light brown, a few shades lighter than before but almost as beautiful as her originals.

They stayed at the cottage for a few days, hardly venturing out. Instead, the caught up with the backlog in lovemaking. On Wednesday, three days after they had arrived at the cottage, at 2.15pm, an unmanned hopper, driven by a robot, arrived in front of the cottage and blew a horn.

Apart from the few clothes that Stephen had sent for them they had no luggage, and they all fitted in a small suitcase.

Nathan opened the hoverer door and helped Lola on board.

"Good afternoon madam and sir! The bar in the back is fully equipped but I would advise you not to drink any alcohol, as the shuttle that will take you to 55 *Cancri 1* will be leaving in three hours."

It was the usual monotonous voice speaking in an universal dialect that usually bored him, but this time it couldn't have made him feel any happier.

"The shuttle journey will be a lot more comfortable if you don't have any alcohol in blood. We will be in New Brighton in forty minutes."

The voyager ship 55 *Cancri 1* weighed couple of teratonnes and was the largest object that humanity had ever constructed. Lifting the parts it needed to the orbit had taken the annual energy output of nations. They would be partaking in one of the greatest enterprises in human history.

What had made star travel possible had been the new mini nuclear reactors, based on an old-fashioned but reliable technology. Combining that with the ability to build unmanned one-way spaceships that carried the radioactive waste to uninhabited radioactive planets within the solar system had silenced the environmental lobby and made virtually unlimited economic growth possible, at least in the Solar Nations. In the last fifty years nuclear energy had become the greenest energy form available. There was plenty of natural radio-activity in the Milky Way; thereby there were plenty of places where to dump the waste, and plenty of uranium could be found within a reasonable distance.

The universe of homo sapiens was slowly expanding, Earth still its centre for the foreseeable future but one day becoming perhaps merely the mythical place of man's origin.

"In the meantime, let me play the introductory video about the destination planet." The robot driver's voice sounded relaxed; there was nothing in its electronic brain, regardless of the fact that it vaguely resembled a man, that obstructed multitasking. This robot didn't suffer from road rage, not even when its initial calculations about the arrival time in New Brighton were now proving optimistic.

The large screen in front of them became alive.

"Your new home, Second Earth, is forty-one light years away. It orbits a star called 55 Cancri that lies in the constellation of Cancer. The journey which will take forty-four years might sound lengthy but that is why the ship has all the possible forms of entertainment and industries anyone can imagine. The size of your apartment is 1,500 square feet, and with three bedrooms, one baby room, kitchen and front room it is one of the largest in the ship. If you decide to sleep through some of or all of the voyage, the apartment has five deep-sleep units which will slow down your biological ageing process by eighty per cent."

Nathan had heard most of this before, but at the time, he hadn't planned to be aboard.

"Imagine; we'll spend almost the rest of our lives aboard."

Lola's voice didn't sound particularly joyful.

"Well, at least there will be thousands of others sharing our destiny, including some friends and family."

"Four of the planets in the system are gas giants similar to

Jupiter, while the innermost planet is believed to resemble Neptune," the introduction continued. "Second Earth will have a beautiful night sky. The planet known before as 55 Cancri f was the first known planet outside our solar system to spend its entire orbit within what we call the habitable zone, a zone where the heat from a star leaves a planet neither too hot nor too cold to support liquid water. Second Earth weighs about forty-five times the mass of Earth and completes one orbit every 260 days. The distance from its star is approximately 72.5m miles, slightly closer than Earth is to the Sun, but it orbits a star that is slightly fainter."

"What is the gravitation force over there, if the planet is so much heavier than Earth?"

The introduction picked Nathan's question. "The gravitation force will be roughly the same, around 1.3G at the settlement. This shouldn't take much adjustment. In fact, apart from the fact that we don't yet know whether the planet has an atmosphere of oxygen already, it is the perfect option for a new home. Also, the gravitation force on the ship will be regulated between 0.9G and 1.1G, so you should be able to feel at home at all times. Also, we believe that, as the planet has a rocky moon there will be liquid water on the surface of the planet. In fact, as far as we know, the 55 Cancri f system is as close to Earth's climate as possible."

"Does it have life?"

"Not as far as we know but the conditions for life do exist, which is more important. It is preferable for life not to exist on the planet, as alien bacteria could wipe out the expedition, even if it didn't encounter any deliberately hostile aliens. It is better to terraform a planet than encounter hostile biosystems."

"Hostile aliens!" Lola, or Melissa said. "I'm looking forward to them."

"The rest of the system consists of a giant planet at 6 AU and four smaller planets inward of 0.8 AU. First, there is a planet the size of Jupiter orbiting close to 55 Cancri and circling it every

14.6 days. Then there is a distant planet, around the distance of Jupiter from Earth with four times the weight of Jupiter. The third planet is about half the size of Saturn, and is orbiting near the star with an orbit time of forty-four days. The fourth planet is hot. It is a planet the size of Neptune-sized planet. The fifth planet is Second Earth."

It would take decades for the star cruiser to make it there.

Yet the presentation was run as if it were a weekend trip.

"What everyone might not know is that 55 Cancri is a double star system," the presentation continued. "Star A is a G8 V yellow dwarf, older and dimmer than the Sun. Star B, 1065 AU from the primary, is a faint M4 V red dwarf. It is around 55 Cancri A that the planets orbit. Many stars with close-in giant planets tend to have high metallicity, and 55 Cancri is no exception. Star A has a metallicity of +0.27, which is 186 times that of the Sun. The star's atmosphere is also rich in carbon compounds, with a ratio of carbon to iron about 141 times that of the Sun. Close in planets have also been associated, at least theoretically, with the phenomenon of super-flares, although super-flares have never been detected from 55 Cancri A."

"Why does Stephen want to go there anyway?" Lola asked.

"The Circle wants to ensure that the expansion of the druidic religion will not spread a corrupt form of the religion. One day, Earth will cease to be the focal point of humanity's existence. The Circle wants to be there, gently guiding the universe toward more peaceful expressions of the religion."

"So, he'll officially be the missionary of the Order but really be there for the Circle."

"Yes. I don't think I really know enough about the Circle to establish what they really stand for but the fact that they saved our lives indicates that at least their intentions might be good."

The hoverer was now approaching New Brighton. Ten minutes later, they joined the queue of fellow travellers. It took them forty-five minutes to get to the Customs.

"Any hand luggage?"

"No."

"It is peak time now, as the ship will be leaving shortly," the officer said. "Most passengers want to leave their lift-off to as late as possible. I mean, it is not as if they'll be seeing any of their family any time soon."

Nathan and Lola smiled.

"Before you go I need to take a sample of your DNA."

"Ok. How much longer until we reach the jump ship?"

"This is the only checkpoint."

A robot official came to take a skin sample.

"That's it. You should be in the jump ship within fifteen minutes. The take-off is in an hour and fifteen minutes. Ever been in space?"

"No," said Lola. "Wanted to go to Mars two years ago but my holiday got cut short."

"Me neither."

"Please go through the security gates. Have a safe journey!"

"Thanks. If we don't like it there, we'll be back in hundred years' time."

"Hopefully, Earth will still be here," the officer said and laughed.

They walked through the gate and a long tunnel that led to the jump ship. The jump ship was already half-full. Nathan estimated that there were around six hundred seats.

An assistant showed them their seats. They looked comfortable but fairly basic.

"The jump will take only about twenty-five minutes, and docking another fifteen," the assistant said. "The connection to the AllNet will be severed for the duration of the journey. That's why there is no entertainment on board. There are some sick bags in front of you in case you feel nauseous. Please fasten your seat belts before the jump."

Nathan sat on the seat and tried to relax. Lola closed her eyes.

"I'm just thinking what the things are I will be missing most," Nathan said. "Oddly, the number one item would be the apple pies baked by Mum. And I don't even remember how they tasted like."

"I'll miss everything," Lola said. "Earth might be polluted but it is still home."

"I will miss nothing," the man sitting next to Nathan said. "I lost my wife and kids in a hoverer crash two years ago. Since then, I have had nothing left on Earth."

"Sorry to hear that."

"Don't be sorry. That's how the wheel of fortune we call life rotates. Why are you heading to the ship?"

"We just want to give our child the best possible future," Lola said.

"So, how will you spend your time on board? The AllNet will be out of reach after we pass Pluto."

"I am sure we will figure something out," Nathan said.

The jump ship's engines came on, and they felt how the body of the ship shook as the engines began to lift the ship upwards, not taking off yet but gaining momentum. It was the last test run before the actual take-off.

The engines shut down and then they switched back on only seconds later. The take-off glued his back on the seat, and pressed the neck backwards forcefully. It was a far from pleasurable experience.

"Quite a ride," the man who sat next to him said.

Nathan doubted that many of the passengers would have been in space before.

Twenty-five minutes later, they were docking onto 55 *Cancri 1*.

Around their docking station he could see other jump ships arriving, and he could recognise the flags of Japan, Korea, Australia and the USA on the sides of the jump ships.

The large screen showed Earth.

"Look! I can see the British Isles!" Lola exclaimed.

"Take one final look."

"The jump ship has now been docked and we are ready to board. Welcome to 55 *Cancri 1* which will be your home for the next forty-five years."

They were in the back of the jump ship and had to wait for their turn before they crossed the bridge to the star cruiser. They got on a little car that drove along the long shopping street that ran through the habitable part of the ship.

"The shopping here should be better than in London," Lola said. "Large parts of the ship have been taken over to manufacturing. We will speed up only after we have pick up some raw materials and ice from the planets. But that will all be done by the shuttles."

"I forgot that you have already been up here."

The vehicle took them to their front door, a journey that took around fifteen minute at twenty miles per hour.

"There are at least one hundred and seventy-five floors. I didn't notice us changing the level," Lola said. "How did they do that? I don't think anyone has their apartment at the entrance level. That's the showcase level for shopping and entertainment."

Nathan pressed his thumb against the scanner. "Welcome, Ethan and Melissa," a cheery female voice said. "It is nice to see you back at home."

The ship was already working hard to make them feel welcome. The door closed after them, and they had the first look at the apartment. It had been decorated in a Japanese style, and its floor was covered with handmade tatami.

"How long did Stephen know that you will be on this ship?" Lola asked. "The apartment has been decorated the way you would have liked it. It's far too perfect to be a coincidence." Nathan was thinking about the same but shook his head. "All I can think is that he has some very powerful friends."

"When did the tatami get installed?" Nathan asked the home system.

"Seventeen minutes ago," the cheerful voice replied. "It arrived in the same jump ship as you did."

"And I thought that Stephen didn't like me," Nathan said in disbelief.

"When will we see him?" asked Lola.

"That might take a while. I suppose by the end of the voyage it wouldn't arouse any suspicions if we were the closest of friends but right now, keeping some distance between us looks like the safest option."

Lola switched on the big screen in the front room.

"Welcome on board! We will now go through a short video about departing from the solar system."

"Why are they in such a rush? We will be stuck here for over forty years," Nathan said.

"It will give them a chance to sell a few more products." Lola said.

"We will be departing tomorrow morning. Our first stop will be at the orbit of Mars where we will be stay for two days to load some cargo and raw materials. If you haven't been in Mars before you will be able to do a day trip on the surface. If you would like to make a day trip please let us know."

"Would you like to do the day trip in Mars?" Lola asked. "I've never been there."

"Mars. We can't go past Mars."

The seer's prophecy flashed through his mind.

"What?"

"I'll explain later. We need to go back to the jump ship dock."

They hired a car and they were back at the dock twenty minutes later.

"The jump ship has already returned to Earth," the station assistant said politely.

"When is the next one?"

"There is no next one. Funny enough, you are the second passenger today that has asked for that. Many passengers seem to already be suffering from home sickness. But don't worry, if you left anything behind, just place an order with the service provider. We will be able to manufacture anything on board. This is a luxury ship, after all."

"OK. By the way, what are these?" Nathan pointed at the AllNet advert playing on the gigantic wall behind the assistant.

"The jump suits. You can hire them before we take off if you want to experience floating in space."

"How safe are they?"

"They have hundred per cent reliability record. You can always press the autopilot button if you feel you're getting lost but most people prefer to stay in control. They are extremely easy to manoeuvre. They can reach the top speed of around one hundred and fifty miles per hour."

"What happens it the engines stop working and you are in danger of crashing to Earth?"

The assistant smiled wryly. "That will never happen. The gravitation force is pretty much no-existing this far from Earth. In the unlikely scenario that you would begin to gravitate towards Earth and the suit wouldn't take you back automatically, it is well capable of dealing with the heat generated by the descent. Also, the parachutes will launch automatically at the height of two miles. You would land safely but obviously, you would miss the voyage, as there are no more scheduled jump ships before our departure."

"Can we book two? Not now but in three hours."

"She will need the maternity model," the assistant said. "That will cost double."

"No problem. It will be the last time when we will ever be able to see Earth from space. It will be well worth it."

"You'll have to sign a waiver. You'll have to be here half an hour early."

They came back two hours later, trying to look as casual and excited as anyone space-floating for the very first time.

First, they had to put on the fireproof undergarment that covered everything but the face; then they were lifted up by straps and lowered into the suit that closed after them.

The suit began to talk to them, giving instructions regarding flying the suit, while a short crane picked them up and began to carry them toward the door that opened.

They were now floating in space, Earth a near-perfect circle below them, the dark space encapsulating them, hugging them.

At least they would be jumping back to Earth and not some unexplored planet.

"How will we override the safety program?" Lola asked through the radio.

"We are not going to override it. We are going to crash it. Or, Edgar will crash it. That's one of those things he's extremely useful for."

"Where is it?"

"It is in the ship. Edgar established contact with me once we came on board. In two minutes, it will crash the safety system, and make these two suits disappear. According to the ship's log, they will have never existed."

"What about the assistant?"

"Forgetting us will be the least of his problems. Whatever he will remember, the system will tell him otherwise."

"Will Edgar be steering us?"

"Yes. He will take us to Nabta Playa."

"So we are not going back to Britain."

"It would be too dangerous. Besides, I have a lot of work to do in Nabta Playa and in Ethiopia. Right now the Outworld, no matter how unsafe it is, is the safest place for us."

Two minutes later, their suits accelerated and began to build distance between them and the ship. Even after a few miles, the ship still looked gigantic, as if they hadn't moved an inch. Then, after around half an hour of flying, the suits began to descend, first slowly, then rapidly. Earth didn't loom much larger yet, but the suit told him that they had reached a speed of three hundred miles per hour. He could see Lola nearby, her falling speed synchronised with his. He could also feel the suit heating up slowly.

Earth looked such a beautiful planet from this distance; there was no hint of the pollution, monstrosities, or any evil things that took place on the planet, every day. If there was a god, or an alien that watched Earth from space, it would have been well pleased with it.

The suit was now heating up considerably, the inside temperature now 89 F°. The suit was monitoring the temperature, not letting it go too high to be harmful to his health but conserving as much energy as possible.

He could now see the ground approaching fast. Then the parachute opened and began to slow down the fall. Minutes later, he crashed on the sands of the Sahara Desert. The crash wasn't that violent but, nevertheless, he fell on the ground, and lay in the sand, until the suit opened automatically and he discarded it like a snake its old skin.

If it had been hot inside the suit, the desert sand felt even hotter. It was afternoon, the hottest time of the day. He got up and walked to Lola who had landed around fifty feet away. He helped her up.

"Are you alright?"

"I am fine. Where can you get some water?"

Nathan pointed at the stone circle that stood at the distance of around half a mile.

"It is fifteen minutes' walk away. The container that was dropped with supplies just a month before we left should still be there."

He took hold of her hand, and they started to walk toward the stone circle.

"I know an old Bedouin not too far from here. He officiates weddings. They are not too bothered about what your religion is as long as you wear a Bedouin outfit. Would you like to get married?"

Lola pressed his hand tightly.

"As long as you don't do it just because of the baby. I'd rather be a single mother."

"I am doing it because if I don't the next Bedouin that sees you will."

The container, around ten feet tall, was still there, its lock unbroken.

"Amazing that no one has broken in," Lola said.

"This is such a god-forsaken place that hardly anyone makes it here. Besides, most locals think the place is haunted."

Nathan went next to one of the megaliths and began to dig. He pulled up a small case.

"Thank gods the lock doesn't work with fingerprint or iris recognition. There is too much sand here for them. It's an old-fashioned lock operated with a key."

He opened the case, and pulled out a long metal key.

"Let's see what we have in here. If I remember right, I stored my desert rat here."

He went to the container that was hot like a frying pan and put the key in the lock.

It screeched but opened.

The desert rat—the little hoverer—was still there. Nathan reached over it to pick up a water canister.

"It might be a bit warm but it should be drinkable."

He opened it and passed it to Lola who drank first.

"It's still the best drink I've had for years."

"We should stay here overnight, and leave very early in the morning before dawn when the heat is still bearable. I have a tent and sleeping bags here. The tent has been designed to keep both the cold and the heat out in the Arctic and Sahara."

He set up the tent close to the container, and they sat inside, waiting for the evening.

It felt like a sauna and Lola's shirt glued to her skin so tightly that he could see her belly button that stuck out because of her bump.

When the night came they slept.

33.

One of Buddha's students asked him, "Are you the messiah?"

"No," Buddha answered.

"Are you a healer?"

"No."

"Are you a teacher?"

"No, I am not a teacher."

"What are you then?" the student asked, exasperated.

"I am awake," Buddha replied.

When Nathan woke up at 3am, he felt awake. Not just because the tent couldn't quite keep out the frost but because the abrupt landing in the desert had somehow woken up his primeval senses. This was a place where much of the information available through the wrist pad was pretty much useless.

He had tested the desert rat in the evening and it seemed to be in full working condition. He had packed some dried food, water, and some guns.

The desert was scarcely populated but not without its dangers. He opened the tent door and looked at the bright night sky. Somewhere out there, there was a planet where Stephen was heading with his family.

He wondered if they had been better off in the ship with its luxuries and easy lifestyle. He knew there was a fair chance that he would never make it back to Britain or London.

With all the work Edgar had done and with all his camouflage, it would still be easy to spot them, and he would always be a fugitive.

He was better off outside the Solar Nations, amongst the people that most citizens of the Solar Nations would perceive as primitive but who still followed ancient codes of honour that made their word much more dependable than most of his friends.

Besides, he had an important task to complete. A task that would take a lifetime.

Staring at the night sky, he looked for the ship, a large enough object to be visible, but he couldn't see it. It might now be visible from New York, as it was the last day before departure. Around fifty-five per cent of the passengers were Americans, looking for a second chance just like their ancestors had done, and the ship was scheduled to be over the American night sky for the departure celebrations.

In many ways, this new adventure of mankind left him sad. The human race was like a plague, invading new territories and raping the land. But perhaps the universe was large enough to be able to withstand the collateral damage inflicted on it by mankind's expansion.

He would never hear what would become of Stephen or his children. Perhaps, some decades or hundreds of years later someone would invent a way to communicate that would be instantaneous but right now, with the speed of the ship near light speed, all the information coming from the ship would be a couple of years old. In forty-five years—if everything went well—they would arrive at the planet that might be habitable but it would take another forty-two years before they would hear about it on Earth.

The families of the first Vikings who went looking for America would never have heard about them again. By the time when it took a month to cross over the Atlantic in a ship the families would get an occasional letter once or twice a year. Then the airplane was invented and suddenly you could cross over the Atlantic in a few hours, and then, people could see each other live with a split second's delay on their computer screens, first two-dimensionally and then three-dimensionally, almost as if their friends and families were on the same room, but alas, if you wanted to touch them it proved to be just an illusion. You could simulate everything else but the human touch and you could even try to simulate that but the simulated human touch wasn't quite the same as the real one. Nothing simulated came even close to his mother's touch, or Lola's touch, or feeling the kick of the unborn baby in her womb.

Lola had woken up, and came sleepily out of the tent, her body warm yet shivering.

"It is time to go."

"Where are we going?"

"First to see the Bedouin who will wed us. Then we will make our way to Ethiopia and to Mediggo. I guess we will be staying there for a few years. Another thing. We should leave our wrist pads behind. Eventually someone will track us down through them. And it is easy to get rid of people here."

"What will we do in Mediggo?"

"I want to get hold of the original book. The one written in the ancient Geez. All the copies have been destroyed but there is still the original. I guess that the seer saw us coming here. I want to complete the translation work. That will take some time, so we need to find ways to make you busy. But first, we need to go to Addis Abeba. There are some decent hospitals there."

Michael McKinley sat by his desk at the Lambeth Palace, when one of his aides came in.

"Any news?"

"No. We established that they travelled under a false identity. Their names are Ethan and Melissa Hawke. They went on board the last jump ship. According to the ship's log, they stayed in their apartment, ordering some supplies on a daily basis. Nothing exceptional. Retrospectively, their behaviour seems far too regimented. It seems someone must have hacked into the central computer and manipulated the information."

"So, where are they now?" Michael asked impatiently.

"We don't know. We sought the ship through with the troops from the Solar Nations when the ship stopped in Mars. No sight of them."

"So what happened?"

"They must have either left the ship or never been there."

"Keep an eye on Stephen. In one sense, if they are still in the ship, the problems they could generate are going further and further away from us. I just feel uncomfortable about the utter incompetence of my staff. With all our budget and access, you can't keep track of two easily identifiable people of which one is pregnant!"

The aide stood there, expecting for more wrath.

"You are dismissed."

The aide turned around and left the room.

Nathan sat next to Lola's hospital bed in Addis Abeba. He held a new-born baby in his arms.

He hadn't imagined that he could ever meet anyone more beautiful than Lola, but there she was.

The most beautiful being in the universe.

She was fast asleep. The window was open, and outside he could hear the hustle and bustle of an Outworld street.

"We're now a proper family," Lola said.

The baby had been five days overdue but the labour had still taken ten hours. It had taken its toll on her but the pain had now left her. She seemed nearly as relaxed as the little baby on his arms.

"Did you know it would be a girl? She looks so pretty."

"Yes I did. I just didn't want to tell you. I wanted it to be a surprise. Have you thought about any names?"

"Her name should be Tikvah."

"I've never heard a name like that. But it is beautiful. Where does it come from?"

"It is Hebrew and it means hope."

"In Yoruba tradition the first child gets seven names. At least one of the names should be Tikvah."

"Alright. With seven names, there won't be any arguments, and she will always be able to choose the one she likes best."

www.ingramcontent.com/pod-product-compliance
Ingram Content Group UK Ltd.
Pitfield, Milton Keynes, MK11 3LW, UK
UKHW041954190726
13854UKWH00005B/1960